FALL
OF THE
WITCHES

THE DATURA CHRONICALS

M.L JEWELL

Angry Night Flower
Press

Edited by: Brittany at BLD Editing

Cover Design by: 3 Crows Author Services LLC

Paperback ISBN: 978-0-6458644-3-4

Ebook ISBN: 978-0-6458644-4-1

CONTENT WARNING

This book contains graphic violence, blood and gore, mention of people being burnt alive and beheaded/executed, coarse language, parental death/murder, sexual content and scenes, child abuse, anxiety/panic attacks, attempted suicide, depression, underage drinking, erotic asphyxiation and the off-scene mention of murdering children.

Some contents within this book may be triggering or disturbing for some readers.

Reader discretion is strongly advised.

To all those who have been made to feel unworthy or like they didn't belong.

Don't give up, you'll find your way.

CHAPTER ONE

MALLRIE

1820

The rhythmic clash of metal echoes through the clearing, bouncing off the rock cliff face like a song. "Mallrie!" a voice booms over the sounds of people sparring. "Again!"

Droplets of sweat race from my brow into my eyes as the early afternoon sun breaks through the trees. My knees quake, and my stomach spasms as I try to force myself back into position. Beads of soil burrow under my nails as my fingers curl into the ground. It's a welcome distraction from the aches in my body. Exhaustion pulls at the edges of my vision, like a loose thread begging to be tugged, threatening me to close my eyes and succumb to it. I no longer want to be in this clearing, my lungs filled with the scent of dirt and sweat. I want to be home, lounging by the fireplace or in bed.

Inhaling deeply, I drop my gaze to my fingers curled in the dirt to avoid the glare of my father. I can still feel his eyes burning into me as I struggle to do another set of push-ups. Gritting my teeth, pain shoots through my jaw from the back of my mouth. Mother says to stop pushing at the tooth, that it'll fall out when it's ready, but the waiting is agonising. I cannot enjoy my favourite dried meat without the pain blooming in my gums. I try to block out everything around me, focusing on breathing like Avark has taught me.

I count each breath.

Whenever a thought pops into my mind, I acknowledge it before pushing it away and restarting my count again.

Every part of me hurts. Mother says they are just growing pains that come along with pushing into young adulthood, but I wonder if I've strained something during the demanding training my father insists on.

Damn. One...two...

The sound of boots crunching against the dirt and dried leaves has me daring to look up, losing track of my breathing once again. My father looms above me. The sun sits behind his head, creating a holy glow like the Fates themselves have blessed him. He's all hard angles and sharp features. He scrubs a hand over his face, over the facial hair that has grown longer than Mother likes. His hair is damp with sweat, the dark tendrils hanging around his face, framing his eyes. He's a handsome man, or so I hear from the gossiping women of our coven. Atherton Delacroix crouches before me, his dark brows slashed over his cerulean eyes. Eyes we share. "What's this?" he asks, smacking my trembling arm.

"I-I'm tired," I grit out, but it sounds like a whine and I flinch, waiting for the reprimand that is sure to follow. *Everything hurts,* I want to add, but I know that won't stop him from making me complete today's training session.

"Don't show your weaknesses, Mallrie." His voice is

solemn, serious. For as long as I can remember, he's told me this. From my first stumbling steps, to getting frustrated when my magic isn't manifesting the way Avark would like, my father always replies with the same four words.

"Don't show your weakness. If people can see where you're hurting, that's where they'll target."

"Don't show your weakness. You're the only heir to the High Witchess. You should be able to control your magic."

Some parents use their words to comfort their children, to tell them it's okay to express their emotions. Mine reminds me to conceal them to protect both myself and my coven. I guess, in a strange way, he's looking out for my well-being in the only way he knows how.

Father's hand presses on the small of my back. "People will exploit your weaknesses if you give them the chance. Do *not* give them the chance, Mallrie. Steel yourself." The extra weight has my body shuddering, my arms a second away from collapsing. "Again!"

No amount of breathing exercises or distractions can pull me back in control of my body. I look inside myself, down that well where my magic manifests, but it feels distant and weak with my exhaustion as I try to call it to my aid. Tears burn at the corners of my eyes.

"I...c-can't," I sob before falling into the dirt. The taste of the earth fills my mouth as I struggle to fill my lungs with enough air to stop myself from panting like a dog in summer. The dirt and mottled grass are cool against my hot skin and remind me that winter is approaching, and these training sessions will end as the sun sets earlier. My father doesn't let me up. His hand presses into the small of my back, and I struggle to calm the panic continuing to rise in me. Everything suddenly feels like it's closing in, and I cannot breathe. Closing my eyes, I try to reassure myself that I will be okay and that I can endure this. Before the panic can find root, my father steps away, releasing me.

"Get up," he snaps, and I scramble to my feet, ignoring my muscles as they scream in protest. I rub my cheek that was pressed against the ground, smearing dirt and sweat across my face. The weight of his gaze has me straightening my spine.

An assessment.

Shoulders back. Chin up.

My heart beats quickly as my father circles me. His eyes narrow slightly as he inspects me, determining my worth. I can't hold the intense scrutiny from him, jutting out my chin, I look past him to focus on the cliffside. I take in every different shade of grey and brown, the small greenery that tries to push its way through the hard and unforgiving rock.

My body jolts forward a fraction as my father claps his hand on my back. "Good job, son. I'm proud of you." There's a hint of a smile peeking out under his thick beard, a glint of pride in his eyes. Praise from my father comes too far and few between, and the panic that was needling at the base of my neck a moment ago has melted into a warm pool in my chest. I feel my eyes burning, tears wanting to form. It's been a while since I've rested, and my body is holding onto every drop of liquid like precious jewels. I am grateful for that. The last thing I need is for tears to line my eyes.

There'll be time to breathe later. Don't show your weaknesses. Steel yourself. Each time I repeat the words, I can hear my father's voice gently guiding me.

"Thank you, sir." I smile, soaking up the attention and paltry words of praise as he ruffles my hair affectionately.

"Go get cleaned up before your mother flays me alive."

CHAPTER TWO

MALLRIE

The further I venture into the Melsheim Forest, the more the thick foliage blocks the afternoon light. I should head in the opposite direction, towards the coven, instead of navigating this narrow path. The trees' unruly roots break through the ground and stumble over each other. An eerie feeling fills the darkness that surrounds me, causing my hand to linger near the pommel of my sword and putting every nerve in my body on high alert.

As nightfall approaches, the overpowering stench of death mingles with that of the forest, pine, and mossy earth. I focus on the latter smell, trying not to think about what is going to emerge once the light fades out completely. I pick up my pace as I race through the forest, jumping over the gnarled roots.

I should bathe in one of the rivers that cut closer to our coven, where it's safer, but I find the quietude of this lake to be far more inviting. Every witchling is taught of the dangers hiding in the pristine waters and how to identify safe swimming locations. While rushing water usually deters merfolk, there's always a possibility of them appearing from the network of tunnels that connect all the water sources. Legend says they're all connected to the Great Lake, deep under the earth's surface, and home to a plethora of precious gems. Many have tried to find the Great Lake, but their bodies have washed up on banks far from where their journeys began, with shredded flesh and missing limbs.

However, the chances that the merfolk would be in this lake are slim, or so I tell myself. The rocky cliffside connects to another source of water—one that I will never venture up to again—but the overflow creates a waterfall that deters the merfolk from entering these waters. The sound of the water cascading down the rock wall creates a calming atmosphere. Wild fruit bushes dot the water's edge, creating an ideal location for birds to flock to indulge in nature's sweet offerings. They must also enjoy the serenity of this place that they too forget about the creatures that lurk in the trees and under the surface because the surrounding trees are alive with the sound of their song, a sweet melody that dances through the air.

This is probably my favourite place in the world. Not that I've ventured farther than the Melsheim Forest. Fates, I haven't even explored a tenth of what the forest holds. The High Witchess restricts how far witchlings can venture into the forest, and some places are even restricted to elders. As it is, this lake would be further than she'd like. So I haven't mentioned this place to my family.

It's a place I can keep all to myself.

Sometimes, when my body aches, this is where I prefer to clean up instead of the brass bath in our home or the rivers the others use after training. Sure, the water can be near freezing, but there's just something about being out here, surrounded by nature and birdsong. If Mother ever found out, facing her wrath would be worth it.

Pushing through the branches, my mind wanders to what Cora is cooking and if I can get a helping before returning home. My stomach growls in agreement, thinking of the pastry I ate this morning before meeting with Avark and training with my father. *Fates, it's been so long since—*

A swooping sensation sweeps through my stomach and my heart stutters, pushing the organ painfully against my ribs like a nightingale in a cage. Despite the ache in my limbs, I lunge behind a nearby tree. A burst of adrenaline races through my body and I clasp my hand over my mouth to smother the sound of my breathing. Every breath, every movement sounds far too loud in my head. I bite down on the inside of my cheek at the haste of my actions.

Living so close to the Melsheim Forest, we're trained to protect ourselves against the creatures that inhabit it. Yet here I am, tears dotting my vision as I glance around the thick tree and spot the juvenile meshlynk drinking from my lake. The meshlynk doesn't look how I expected it to, given the illustrations in the tomes and the stories we're told.

The broken blisters on my hand throb as my grip tightens around the leather handle of my sword. The scrape of metal feels too loud in my ears as I gradually inch the weapon out of the sheath. The meshlynk sinks its large claws into the damp earth as it tilts its head, dropping the hood of shrubbery and antlers that grow from its shoulders. I tuck myself back against the broad tree to avoid its red-eyed gaze.

The suffocating grip of dread tightens in my chest at the

thought of being ensnared in the meshlynk's psychic manipulation. Stories of people getting trapped in their own minds as the creature forces them to murder, then sacrifice themselves play into my growing fear. My breathing becomes erratic. The intensity of my hold on the sword causes my palm to pulse with each beat of my heart. My magic thrums under my skin, warning me of my dangerous surroundings, as if I don't already know. It buzzes around me like hornets, causing the hairs on my arms to stand, slipping through my veins like water through my fingers as I lose control. I watch in shock as a clawed hand slowly emerges from my left and reaches around the huge trunk. I can hear the bark splinter as the dirt-and-moss-encrusted claws sink inch by inch into the tree.

Sucking in a mollifying breath, I step out from behind the trunk, swinging my sword. The hiss of the metal sings through the air as it falls on the neck of the meshlynk. The creature lets out a blood-chilling sound, a mix between a hiss and a snarl. My magic shudders and crackles up my arms, and time resumes its regular pace. The meshlynk's sharp claws snap out, gripping me around the throat. Its horrid face inches closer to mine, emitting a gurgling hiss that sends shivers down my spine. Desperately trying to avoid eye contact, I focus on the dribble of blood and saliva seeping from the corner of its mouth. With a shaky hand, I lift my sword and awkwardly swing it, hacking haphazardly at the arm. Sinking its claws into my throat, the meshlynk's fingers splay, dropping me to the ground. Roots jabbing me in the back, I waste no time as I swing a leg, sweeping the creature off its feet. My head aches from the impact as I stand, my vision spinning as I swing my sword in my hand, just as I've seen my father do in training many times before. *Maybe he does it to distract his opponent from seeing where they've injured him.* The blade pierces deep into the creature's chest. Blood splatters on my clothes and dots against my skin as I stand over the meshlynk, panting hard.

CHAPTER THREE

MALLRIE

The chill of the lake clings to my body, immovable as I race against the setting sun. My breath lightly clouds before me as my boots pound into the dirt and propel me over fallen branches. Icy droplets race down my neck and into the collar of my shirt. Thoughts of enormous bonfires and roasted nuts fill my mind, my magic drawing on and bringing those memories of the past winter festivals to life around me.

My magic skitters along my skin. I can practically hear the lively music and smell the crisp, wintry air and roasted nuts drizzled with honey. It's a pleasant distraction from my filthy clothes, covered in sweat, dirt and the blood of the juvenile meshlynk. Normally, I wash my clothes before going home. But after the encounter with the creature, every nerve in my body is on high alert, and my instincts urge me to return to the safety of the coven. A whine builds at the back of my throat, knowing that I'll have to wash them later. Cleaning my clothes is not something I enjoy. It's such a mundane chore and one that my mother insists I do myself.

My hand finds the hilt of my short sword. I push through the aches in my body, forcing myself to go faster through the forest towards the familiar glow of the Enkantian Coven. As the sun begins its descent, another deadly predator will prowl these woods. I may have bested the meshlynk thanks to the will of the Fates, but I doubt they'd bless me with a victory against a Kailadon. Though their appearance may be deceiving, these nocturnal creatures are far deadlier than most others within the forest. A shudder courses down my spine at the thought of their insatiable hunger for flesh—and worse, their great, bladed arms.

Father has mentioned that next month, once winter has well and truly dug her frozen claws into the earth and the sun falls behind the forest earlier, we'll venture into the forest, and I'll finally see firsthand what the Kailadons are capable of and how to defend myself against them.

A swell of pride fills my chest as I remember his praise from earlier, and I get a spark of hope that I may get another clap on the back or some words of encouragement that I can lock away and remind myself when my magic isn't manifesting the way Avark would like, or my body cannot keep up with the other warriors. I slaughtered a juvenile meshlynk all on my own, walking away with only a few pinpricks on my throat.

The golden, honeyed glow of the coven breaks through the trees and I slow to a jog, running my hand through my damp hair, my stomach growling uncomfortably. My mind drifts to the warm, comforting thoughts of what Cora has simmering over the fire at the moment.

Weaving between the cabins, I politely smile and wave as I pass people. The weight of their stares hangs heavily on my shoulders as my mother's words ring through my mind.

"One day, Mallrie, I'll step aside. You'll become the High Witch and will have to protect your people."

I am proud to be the first-born son of the High Witchess, Cersei Delacroix, but with this honour comes sacrifices.

The tempting scent of wild mushroom and deer stew fills the air the closer I get to Cora and Lia's home. Cora is, in my opinion, the best cook in the coven. She's definitely better than my mother (not that I'd ever give voice to that thought). Plus, she always has fresh bread and pastries that she indulges me with. The latter treats are never available at home, and even if they are, Father wouldn't allow me to indulge. Cora, on the other hand, will sneak treats into my jacket pockets. My knuckles rap against the wooden door as I poke my head in and call out to her. Her laughter fills me with a warmth I am still getting used to. My chest feels tight at the sound, and yet there's a lightness that pulls an unstoppable smile from my lips. It's a sound that isn't heard often in my home. For as long as I can recall, there has always been a strong sense of structure in the Delacroix home.

"Come in, little Mallrie," Cora calls from deep within the small, one-bedroom house. "I was wondering when you'd show your ruddy little face."

I'm offended by the suggestion that I'm just a child playing in the mud all day. "Father had me stay back at training," I say, falling onto one of the many feather-filled pillows stacked in the corner by the window, reminding her

I was doing something of importance. Exhaustion washes over me as I fluff up a pillow under my arm and sink further into its softness. "Then there was this juvenile meshlynk near the—"

"Please tell me—" Cora steps out from behind the wall, her brown eyes blowing wide when she notices my blood-covered clothes. "Mallrie..." she breathes, wiping her hands on her cotton apron, as she crosses the room and drops onto her knees before me, concern filling her tone. "Please tell me you didn't fight it." Her viciously scarred hands sift through my hair.

I flash her a smile as she tilts my face one way, then the next. "I killed it, Cora!"

She examines the marks on my throat. "He's putting too much pressure on you," she whispers to herself. I study her face, trying to figure out the reason behind the sadness and longing in her voice. Her fingers linger on my neck, gently caressing.

"I can handle it, though." I beam up at her, straightening myself. "Training has been a part of my life for as long as I can remember!" Pride fills my chest as I palm the sword sitting beside me. The kids my age are only just starting their training, and most of them have never stepped foot in the forest alone. But my father has been teaching me how to yield a sword—albeit a wooden toy—since I could walk. Eventually, that play fighting turned into racing through the forest, climbing over fallen trees and large rocks. Father would reason that it was to get some of my excess energy out before bed, but I can see the ways he was subtly readying me for when I was old enough to train.

Cora runs a hand through her dark hair. "You're still a child, Mallrie. You should be out there playing, not running around pretending to be your father." There's a hint of disdain in her voice. "I don't understand his obsession with teaching you to fight."

"Why shouldn't I learn to fight?" I ask, confusion settling across my brow. "The creatures out there won't care whether I can or cannot defend myself. They won't spare me just because I am a child." The word feels almost insulting on my tongue. *Cora is right. I have little experience playing, but I find it pointless.*

Her jaw tightens. "You *are* a child. A lot can be learned through playing. You're too young to be taking life so seriously." Her eyes drop to the sword at my side. "And you know the rules about weapons inside." She raises a dark brow and flicks a finger towards the door.

I push myself off the pillows with a muted groan, my muscles screaming out in pain. I mutter an apology as I head to place the blade outside.

Pushing open the door, I call out to Cora, who's already returned to the kitchen. "Besides, Leander has been training since he could walk!" Now he's one of my father's favoured warriors. Though our coven hasn't seen war for fifty years, it's something still fresh in the elders' minds. The last one our coven saw was against the lorkreigs. It wasn't a terribly long or destructive war, unlike that between the Enkantian and Wincroft covens when they fought for the misnacs, which ended in the extinction of the magical cats.

A rough laugh echoes around the sound of simmering pots and clanging spoons. "Leander didn't touch steel until he was twelve, and even then, he almost lost his hand."

Leaning against the wall near the kitchen, knowing full well to never step inside when Cora is cooking, lest I want a wooden spoon to fall across my knuckles, I say with smug satisfaction, wiggling my fingers, "Well, looks like I am already better than Leander."

Cora laughs and ruffles my short black hair. "I'm staying out of that debate."

Which is fair, I think, considering Leander is her twin. Before I can speak, Lia storms into the warm home, cursing and knocking the mud from her boots.

"Lia Le Torneau! Language!" Cora snaps, a wooden spoon clanging against the side of the pot, drawing attention to her displeasure. "There is a child present."

"I'm not a child!" I protest. "I am almost eight!"

Lia laughs, calling out to her wife, "Sorry, my love." She gives me a mischievous look, whispering, "You know that curse, don't you?"

My cheeks redden as I nod silently. It's hard not to know it when I'm training with Lia and the other Enkantians almost every other day.

"Weapons outside!" Cora sighs just as Lia has finished hanging up her jacket, having dumped her weapons on the small kitchen table. "You'd swear we live like swine."

Lia wraps a muscular, tattooed arm around Cora's waist, pulling her closer. "I'm sorry, my love." She kisses Cora's shoulder. "It's been a long day." She sighs, kissing her neck. I turn my attention to setting the table. "Unsuccessful hunt. There was..." Lia's voice trails off, and she glances in my direction. "I'll tell you about it later," she whispers, kissing Cora quickly before taking her long bow and short Dane axes outside to hang on the wall.

Meals with the Le Torneaus are my favourite. As much as I love my parents, there is just something different about meal times here. Perhaps it's because Lia and Cora allow me to engage in their conversation, asking for my thoughts and feelings instead of talking over me and pretending as if

I'm not there. Or maybe it's the playfulness that is Lia stealing Cora's honeyed carrots off her plate because she always wants more than Cora serves her. There's no doubt in my mind that my parents love me, but there's some sense of separation between the three of us that I don't feel here with Cora and Lia.

I listen to the two women share about their day. Cora fills Lia in on the gossip from the other women in the coven that was shared while washing clothes and skinning pelts.

"Miles asked if I could fill in for his class next Hydrus Day."

My head picks up. *That's only four days away.* "Can I come?"

Cora smiles sweetly, yet I can see the sadness in her eyes. "I haven't said yes yet, Mallrie."

"Why not?" Lia asks, dipping her bread in the stew. "It would be great for you to practise again, and not just the meandering little bits and pieces you do around the home."

Cora looks down at her arm, at the burns that cover her from fingertips to elbows. "I'm not sure if I'm prepared for that yet."

I drop my eyes to my bowl of stew. A wave of awkwardness washes over me, a flush creeping across my face like I shouldn't be here for this conversation. My spoon scrapes across the surface of the stew as I try to make myself smaller and unnoticeable like I've done from time to time when my parents have a tense conversation. Even though Cora has never shied away from answering my questions, I know it's a difficult topic for her to talk about.

"My love, you can't keep hiding in the kitchens."

I look up to see Lia gripping Cora's arm, her pale thumb lovingly brushing against the dark, rough skin. The gesture is so small, but I can see how much it means to Cora. It's in the tears that dot the corners of her eyes and the way her shoulders relax a fraction. "Don't get me wrong, we love your cooking. Right, Mal?"

"Oh, Fates, yes!" I exclaim, craning my neck towards the kitchen. "You made those apple turnovers, right?"

"Of course," Cora says, her voice filled with laughter. She lifts my hand and places a kiss on my knuckles, sending a wave of butterflies fluttering through my body to rest on my chest. Cora and Lia are so openly affectionate and share their love with all those around them.

"Your magic is strong, my love, but you're stronger," Lia says, kissing Cora's hand. "Love yourself enough to learn to control it."

Cora's lip wobbles, her glassy eyes dropping to the table as she says, "I'm trying to, but there's a difference between summoning a flame to cook a loaf of bread and teaching a bunch of bright-eyed witchlings how to control something that is very dangerous."

"You won't hurt them," I say, dropping my spoon in my bowl. "You've shown me how your magic works countless times and never hurt me."

"But accidents happen, Mallrie." she sighs sadly. "And people can get hurt."

"But hiding yourself and restricting your magic will not protect those you love," Lia says, looking at me, but the statement is clearly pointed at Cora.

My chest feels tight as Cora twists the simple metal band on her finger. "What if I cannot control it?" she whispers, emotion clogging her throat.

Lia places a hand over Cora's, her thumb brushing over her scarred knuckles. "I believe in you. *We* believe in you."

Cora's lips wobble as I nod, because I *do* believe in her. She's shown me some amazing tricks she can do with her magic. She's truly talented. Cora slips her hands out from under her wife's and places them in her lap under the table. "What if *I'm* not ready? What happened was..." her voice trails off, but Lia is already there.

"Cora, what happened was horrible, and a tragic accident. Everyone knows that. I understand there's... trauma and anxiety that come along with it, but do you really think hiding away baking is the best way to deal with it? Practising your magic, sharing your story with the witchlings, *teaching them* what can happen if they're not careful... isn't that better?"

Cora and Lia are both silent. They sit there, staring into each other's eyes as Lia slips her hand under the table. I look away, feeling uncomfortable being here in such an intimate moment.

"Though we appreciate it," I blurt out. "The baking, I mean, and the apple turnovers," I add, reminding them of the delicious pastries in the other room.

Lia barks a laugh as Cora's smile softens, her hand ruffling my hair. "I'll think about it, okay?"

"Can I come?" I ask again.

"If I agree, you *must* be there."

The smile that lights my face fills my heart with hope. "Front row, Cora."

CHAPTER FOUR

MALLRIE

"**M**allrie!" Leander calls from his seat outside the tavern, nearly knocking over his tankard as he lifts his hand in greeting. "What's Cora cooking tonight?"

"Not enough for you!" I call back, earning a chorus of laughter from his friends as they whack him on the back in faux torment. *I don't think my remark was that witty.* My footsteps falter. Despite my exhaustion and the allure of my cosy bed and a warm mug of lavender tea and Cora's sweet ginger biscuits, I find myself hesitating near the tavern. And despite having Avark's assignment still sitting untouched on my desk, I linger near the building under the light of the moon and the twinkling stars, jeering with Leander.

Just for a moment.

"How'd you go today?" he asks, changing the subject.

I huff a laugh and wander closer to the tavern than I probably should. "Not as good as I'd have liked." *Well, as my father would have liked.*

"Ah, you'll get there, mate," Leander says, as if hearing those unspoken words, leaning on the table. "Tomorrow,

I'll give you a few pointers that'll really impress Atherton, alright?"

He winks as I nod my thanks and repress a sigh at having to continue home. I pass the large oak tree in the centre of our coven, looking up at the tiny fireflies buzzing around the branches like the stars in the sky. There's something magical about Vaasis on an evening like this. The moonlight filtering through the branches and the enchanting dance of fireflies could make anyone's troubles simply melt away.

My magic presses against my skin, buzzing like hornets as I approach our home, but I'm too exhausted to heed its warning. The magic within Vaasis protects our coven. It even spreads into the Melsheim Forest. There's no danger here. It leaks from my skin, sending a shudder down my spine, and the good, warm feelings of spending time with Cora and Lia leak away as time slows.

Each creak and whine of the hinges sounds too loud in my head as I push open the door. Flames dance across the hearth and fill the room in their warm, golden glow, illuminating my mother's light brown hair as it falls in waves around her waist. She's frozen, and a breath pushes from my chest as I wonder if I have frozen time completely. Overwhelmed by panic, I find myself anchored in the doorway, my mind racing through the potential punishments that Avark may inflict upon me for stopping time. His raspy voice echoes in my head, long lectures of the effects and consequences of freezing time, even momentarily, playing out. The repercussions of tempting the Fates. My hand flexes at my side, the welts on my knuckles aching with the movement.

It'll be okay. I try to focus on my breathing, to calm my nerves and regain control of my magic. Remembering

Avark's lessons, I close my eyes and reach out for it. In my mind's eye, I picture the room, and slowly, purple, misty tendrils appear, snaking around the space and ensnaring it. The mist trembles as I call it back, eventually retreating.

With an exhale, relief washing through me and a whoosh of magic, time resumes its normal pace. The flames resume their flickering, a bead of wax slides down the candles on the wall sconces and the curtains flutter in the evening breeze.

Yet, my mother is still unmoving.

The light of the fire shimmers along her emerald gown. My heart skips a beat as I wonder what she's holding in her arms; it's capturing all of her attention. My fingers flex around the hilt of my sword, but I don't sense any danger in the room, even with Mother's rigid posture. My boots hardly make a sound as I walk across the room. *Heel then toe.* Just as Lia and Leander have taught me, I move silently as a wraith. As I push onto my toes to see what is swaddled in her arms, I accidentally knock over an urn of flowers. The metal clashes against the floor, my mind too distracted to reach out with my magic to catch it.

Yet, Mother doesn't flinch.

Her eyes are fixated on the bundle in her arms, her body frozen as I move around to step in front of her. Her eyes are dark and glaring down at—

"Is that a baby?" I ask, taking a step closer and placing my arm on my mother's, trying to get a better look.

I have always wanted a sibling. Preferably a brother I can train with, but I'd also love a sister. Someone to love and teach, to protect.

Mother has told me that all the children in the coven are like my brothers and sisters, and when I become High Witch, it is them who I'll turn to for support. Yet, when I've tried to converse and play with them, it's never filled me with that warmth I see when they engage with their *actual* siblings. The way they play and fiercely protect each other. It's as if they indulge me out of obligation.

There is an immovable loneliness in my chest. My heart stammers as I push onto the tips of my toes to get a better look.

My mother looks down at the swaddled babe in her arms. "It would appear so," she says sternly, her face twisting into a grimace.

How could she look at a baby that way? With such disdain and hatred?

"This is Cyan, your new baby *brother*," she spits, turning and pressing the bundle into my arms. He is heavier than I expect, and my arms shake under his weight. His face scrunches up, and soon his soft cries turn into wails that could awake the dead. My throat constricts as I look down at his reddening face. I look to Mother for help, but she just rolls her eyes and looks back to the fire, rubbing at her temples. I carefully jiggle Cyan, attempting to recreate the motion I've seen other mothers do when their babes are distressed. It does little except loosen the swaddle. I shift his weight in my already aching arms, my determination to keep him safe strengthening me.

"Are you not happy to have another son, Mama?" I gently brush the rough wool blanket away and run my finger down his ruddy little face. His face is red and splotchy from crying, but it's the smear of dirt around his jaw and ears that confuses me. He's so little, too little to be playing around in the dirt. Cyan wiggles in my arm, and the thought of dropping him has my magic reacting instinctively, slowing down time so I can readjust my grip. A small hand wraps around my finger, and all that panic and fear simply melt away as Cyan guides it into his mouth to suck. I jerk it away, unsure if babies should suck on other people's fingers. I know they suck on their own hands to soothe themselves, but I've never seen them suck on someone else's. Given, I have paid little attention to babies. I look down at my hands. Though I scrubbed them as best as I could at Cora's before dinner, dirt still lingers under my nails, and my skin is rough and broken from training. Not at all appealing for a small child to soothe themselves with. A slight frown presses at my brows, and I can't help but wonder again how my mother could look at someone so sweet and innocent with such... hatred.

She walks over to the small wooden table. "I'd be honoured to have another son," she murmurs, uncorking a bottle with a *pop* and filling her silver goblet with wine. Mother's green eyes lift to where I still stand, gently rocking Cyan. "But that *bastard* is no son of mine," she seethes from around the goblet. Her eyes are hard and cold, and she stares unseeingly at the baby as she drinks deeply.

"Bastard?" I don't understand the context, although I've heard Leander call his friends this in good faith while training together. But the way Mother says it sounds strange, the word filled with loathing and betrayal.

Cyan opens his eyes, looking at me with eyes so similar to mine. Our father's eyes. "I don't understand, Mama."

His eyes grow heavy as he sucks on my finger despite my best efforts to stop him, and he drifts off to sleep again.

"You don't need to, my dearest." Mother crosses the room and presses an unusually rough hand against my shoulder. I can smell the liquor on her breath. A part of me, deep inside, has my grip tightening on the bundle. The anger in her eyes makes me nervous, a feeling that is entirely unjustified, because my mother would hurt no one.

As the High Witchess of our coven, she's sworn an oath to hold the livelihoods of her coven above her own.

"Just promise me you'll take care of him." Her voice is a desperate slur. I want to ask why she cannot look after my brother. *Is she going somewhere? Of course I'll protect him.* But that isn't what she meant. As she turns her back on us, I know that down to my bones. Before I can open my mouth and ask the questions I'm desperate to find answers for, my father's voice rings in my mind. *"A Delacroix always keeps their promise."*

I look down at the babe, finally settled back to sleep in my arms. "I promise, Mama."

And I will protect him no matter what.

CHAPTER FIVE

MALLRIE

1838

The low whistle is my only warning before the sound of wood on flesh echoes in the cave. My body jerks, and I swallow a curse that's poised on the tip of my tongue —several curses, in fact—but I keep them locked behind my clenched jaw. Avark stands before me, leaning casually on his cane, his dark hair pulled back, streaks of grey forming around his temples and in his moustache. "Focus now," he grumbles, tapping the cane on the wooden desk where I'm painstakingly deciphering ancient scriptures. Scriptures that are tucked into the hollowed-out rock in the walls amongst carvings, symbols and enchanted fires flickering in sconces along the walls, lighting the small space.

This place was carved into the southern hillside of the coven by my father at Avark's request. It's warded to protect the outside world against our magic. *"Time is a fickle thing,"* Avark told me when he first brought me here. *"We're tempting the Fates when we look into the* Timeline.*"* The *Timeline* is a web of possibilities weaved by the Fates' ancient hands. If someone were to stumble upon a future possibility, it could have detrimental effects.

Avark and my father worked together to enchant the entrance to contain the magic and prevent others from entering the cave. The invisible barrier only allows Avark, Father and me to pass through, but it doesn't shield the small cave from the changing seasons. The summer heat is almost unbearable, making it difficult to find relief and concentrate. And in the winter, the cold is bone-chilling, making you long for warmth. There's only a tiny window through the seasons where the only suffering you have to endure is Avark's lessons.

I bite back the words poised on my tongue. *How am I meant to focus when so much is going on? When just beyond here, everyone is still celebrating the birth of my sisters? When Cyan is no doubt passed out somewhere or still celebrating?* A spear of jealousy stabs through me at the freedom he's offered. He's not held down by the coven's expectations of him. He's free to learn and train however he pleases.

Avark clears his throat and I drop my eyes to the page before me, letting my magic thrum to the surface, attempting to bring some semblance of clarity to the scribbles. Sweat drips down my spine from the concentration and the humidity in the enclosed cave.

I flick open the leather satchel next to my stool and pull out an apple, Avark having returned to his desk to read through the assessment I handed in. I take a bite. Its sweet juices sweep over my tongue and I set it before me on the table, shifting the scripture to the side to keep it out of the way. Magic surges through my body, racing through my veins to my hands, where I motion the spell, summoning the essence of time itself.

Forefingers touch, thumb... flip. Push.

Slowly, the apple rots.

Avark looks up from where he's grading my paper. "Impressive, Mallrie. But you were required to turn it back into a seed."

I hold my tongue, biting back the remark that's poised there. If I let it loose, Avark will only keep me here longer, and I can already hear the faint cheering and the *whoosh* of the bonfire being lit. The celebrations are getting underway, and I am *missing* them. My jaw grinds together as I look from the rotten apple to where Avark is crossing out line after line on my assessment.

"Sir," I clear my throat, trying to calm my voice. "Can we pick this up later? I cannot miss the festivities."

Avark doesn't look up from the papers. "The celebrations are going on for three nights, Mallrie. One night to honour each child." His eyes peer over his spectacles. "You were in the midst of the celebrations last night. I'm sure you can miss *one* night of drinking and merriment for your education?"

My hands ball into fists as I push to my feet. "Respectfully, sir—"

My mouth loses the words and instead fills with a rotten taste of bile. My muscles constrict as I am forced back into my seat, and I watch as my fists unclench against the wooden surface. "You were already late for your lesson. Do you not recall?"

"Yes, sir." The words push through clenched teeth as he manipulates time. *Surely, the Fates frown upon this.* My stomach still recoils at the way Avark used his magic to pull the lingering alcohol from my body when I arrived this afternoon, half drunk and not at all determined to focus on the tasks he set before me.

He glares at me over his spectacles, challenging me

again. I keep my mouth shut against the words I wish to speak. Lifting his quill, he points at the apple on my desk. "Try that again, Mallrie."

We stare at each other for a tense moment before I drop submissively, knowing that it was a threat rather than a request.

CHAPTER SIX
CYAN

Fire and earth elementals work together, sending balls of fire infused with pigments from botanicals into the sky. They explode in bursts of colour—red, orange, purple and blue. My feet linger where some earth elementals are producing flowers for the display. Balling my hand, I shove it deep into my pocket to stop myself from reaching out to help.

The coven treats me... differently.

Mallrie tries to shield me from their stares and murmurs, but I see them. Worse, I hear what they say.

"He's a little strange, don't you think?"

"There's something... off about his magic."

Mal tells me that they've said the same things about him in the past. I don't believe him. They look at him as if he hung the moon.

I weave my way through the crowds, not exactly sure where I am going, but I don't feel like I belong here. Since the birth of Alinta, Adriana and Abeline, Mother has been exhausted and irritable, so I've been trying to keep to the shadows whenever I'm at home. The coven has adorned the front of our house with garlands and small lanterns, illuminating the enchanted flames in shades of pink, white and green. They created intricate swirling designs at the entrance using coloured pebbles, and on top of them, three wooden bassinets sit, filled with soft silk. Mother sits on an upholstered chair, her neatly piled hair atop her head, the soft gown she's wearing slouching down one arm as she feeds one of the girls. Another is crying in the bassinet and Father is nowhere to be found—or Mallrie, for that matter.

The breath I suck in feels like it's laced with tiny fragments of ice as I step up beside the bassinet with an *A* carved on it—a good lot of help that is when all three girls' names start with the same letter. I scoop up the small baby; Adriana, I think. It's hard to discern since they're all identical.

"I can take her," Mother says, holding out her free arm.

"I don't mind," I whisper, tightening the swaddle around Adriana and gently swaying from side to side. Her cries soften as she settles in the crook of my arm, her head rolling into my chest as she falls back to sleep.

"You'll spoil her if you let her sleep in your arms like that," Mother snaps, her tone sharper than Enkantian steel.

My smile fades as Mother's words pierce my chest. It's a dismissal—one I've heard many times since the girls' birth. I return Adriana to her bassinet. Her small, pink face scrunches up and her lip quivers, shattering my heart. *I don't think letting her sleep in my arms would spoil her. It's a comfort that she's missing. She's used to being with her sisters inside the womb.*

But what would I know?

"Let me know if you need any—"

"I need nothing from you, Cyan."

I bow my head and stalk off, hearing Adriana's cries start up once more.

CHAPTER SEVEN
MALLRIE

As soon as Avark dismissed me, I was out of that stuffy cave faster than a flash of lightning. I hastily dumped my books and quills into my satchel, and slung it over my shoulder without hesitation.

The possibility of the pot of ink spilling is high, but I don't care right now. I can always practise that spell Avark had me doing with the apple to remove the stains. The fallen leaves crunch beneath my boots as I manoeuvre around, gripping onto the sturdy trunk of a nearby tree. I can faintly hear the chorus of laughter and frivolity of the coven celebrating. I want to get home, drop off my satchel and change my shirt before joining in on the festivities, but as soon as I make it to the edge of the forest and see the coloured flames the fire elementals have enchanted, I just want to see my baby sisters and get a drink with my brother.

Most people acknowledge me with a smile or a simple nod, allowing me to pass without trying to strike up a conversation. I keep my head down and my pace quick. I can see our home on the other side of Vaasis, but it's Leander's laughter that has my footsteps faltering. He's sitting at his favourite table at the tavern, his dark hair pulled back at the nape of his neck and the sleeves of his tunic rolled to his elbows, exposing black ink. The laughter from his friends dies down as I walk by. Despite Leander calling out to me, I want to just slip away, feeling like I'm intruding on something I am not welcome to.

"Where have you been?" he asks.

"Studying with Avark," I reply, shifting my satchel on my shoulder. "Apparently, no celebration is too important to stop learning." My chest feels tight as Leander's friends lean in to each other and continue talking. "I'll leave you to it."

He pushes from his stool and jogs to catch up, dropping his arm around my shoulders. "Don't worry about them, Mal."

"I'm not," I reply. As kind as Leander has always been—being one of the few people who'd train with the sole heir of the High Witchess—there's always felt a strain there. Especially as I've grown. Where Cyan and I grew closer in age, it feels Leander and I have grown apart.

"Ah, they're alright, mate," he says, glancing over his shoulder at his friends drunkenly laughing in the distance. "They're just trying to have a good time."

"Then go have a good time with them, Leander. Like I said, I'm fine. They're your friends. They've made it clear in the past that you're my friend, and that there's a distinguishable line between the two." They have never outwardly said so. But there's always been the inside jokes that I was not privy to because of my age, or the fact that I wasn't around for those hunting trips. And that was always fine. I never let it get to me. But sometimes, it was hard growing up, because it felt like I was suspended in time.

Too young to go hunting with Leander and his friends, but too old to play with the kids my age because of the training my father and Avark insisted on. It wasn't until Cyan was about thirteen that I truly felt like I had someone I could connect with.

"Mate, you know that's not true. You're welcome to grab a drink with us any time."

A smile forms on my face, one that I have adopted after watching my mother's interactions with the coven when her patience is waning. "I know. I'm only fucking with you." *I absolutely am not, but now isn't the time or place for this.* "It's just been a long morning and I'm pissed at Avark for keeping me so long."

Leander laughs, and it's almost identical to his sister, Cora's, which fills my heart with a warmth I miss some days. "That's fucking fair, mate. That old crone is a rotten bastard. I remember when Cora and I were kids and she lost control of her magic, trying to light a lantern so we could sneak out to watch the Vaasis ritual." I flinch, knowing how this story ends. "Cora's hands..." Despite the copious amounts of liquor I imagine Leander has consumed, he seems to have sobered at the memory. "They were messed up. There's a reason witchlings who possess fire magic are to keep their practices in controlled environments until they're in their first decade of life, you know?"

My stomach twists. Leander has conveniently left out the part where Cora severely burnt his legs as well as her own hands in the process. But he's never been one to dwell on that fact or to hold it against her. It was an accident. Everyone knows that.

But my stomach is in knots for another reason. Avark checked the *Timeline* when Mother gave birth to see what elemental magic the girls would develop. Adriana is a fire

34

elemental, and I worry about how she'll go, controlling her magic. The last thing I'd want is for her to go through what Cora did.

"We didn't want our parents to find out what happened. So we snuck out and found Avark after the ritual. Fucking bastard wouldn't do anything to help her. Said it was a *fucking lesson*."

"Sounds like Avark," I mutter, clenching my fist at my side and feeling the stretch of skin over my knuckles. I don't need to look to know that they've started to swell.

Leander clears his throat. "Anyway, Cor's learnt how to cope... sort of."

"Mm, sort of," I agree under my breath. I remember the time Cora taught Miles' class. She struggled to get through the lesson and opted to do more of a theoretical-based lesson than the hands-on lesson Miles had planned for her. She cried for hours afterwards, and I didn't know whether to stay with her or go find Lia.

"Anyway," —Leander claps me on my back, snapping me out of my stupor— "you're free now. Put your stuff away and come grab a drink with us."

I agree to get a drink with him later, even though I know I'll just be grabbing two bottles of wine and slipping away to find Cyan. Maybe I'll find some girls to join us. Fates know I need some sort of distraction after my lesson with Avark this morning.

Mother is sitting outside our home under the coloured firelight, a rare moment when all three girls are asleep.

"How have they been?" I ask, slipping my satchel off my shoulder and onto the floor beside one bassinet with a carved *A*.

"Needy," Mother says, tilting her head back and closing her eyes. "It wasn't like this with you," she mutters, a small smile tugging at her lips.

"Ah. Well, you see, there was only one of me." I bite my tongue, stopping the crude comment about how if she had three sons to begin with, she'd have removed Father's manhood before he could sire any more children.

When she doesn't reply, and I've checked to make sure there's still three perfect, healthy little girls asleep in their bassinets, I move to my mother's side. "Where's Father?" I ask. "Has he gone to get you something to eat or drink?"

"I would assume he's out celebrating himself." The words are clipped. Father didn't want to be present during the birth. After witnessing it myself, I don't blame him. But she is his wife, and she was birthing his children. He should have been there. Thankfully, Cora was with me. All I had to do was change out washcloths and then hold my sisters, who were so much smaller than Cyan was, though he was a lot older when I first held him.

"I'll get you something to eat," I say, pressing a kiss to her brow before slinging my satchel inside the door.

"That's not where that goes, Mallrie," Mother chides, still with her eyes closed and head resting back.

I smirk. Though she can't see it, there's no doubt she can hear it in my voice. "I'll put it away later."

CHAPTER EIGHT

CYAN

"Cyan!"

The tension I didn't know had formed in my shoulders releases at the sound of my name. Only Mallrie could make that tension leave my body with a shout of my name. Turning, I find him running towards me, two ales spilling over the brims of their tankards.

"Blessed Fates, you're a sight for sore eyes!" I exclaim, taking the jug from his outstretched hand and drinking deeply. The ale slips across my lips and dribbles down my chin. It's perfectly sweet with a hint of fruity tones.

Mal chuckles darkly. "You sound like you need this just as much as me." His fingers tip the tankard higher, encouraging me to keep going.

I choke on the last of the ale, coughing and pushing Mal away from me through my laughter. "You fucking *look* like you need it," I say through my coughing and laughing fit. "Training that bad, eh?"

Mallrie's hand flexes at his side as he takes a large gulp of his ale. "You could say that."

"I did say that, and that's not an answer."

Mallrie's lips curve into a smirk. "You're too smart for your own good sometimes, you know that?"

"Yeah, I'm a bloody genius. Now answer the question," I say with a pointed glance at his swollen knuckles.

"What's there to say?" Mallrie tosses his arm over my shoulder, leading me through the crowds of people dancing. "Avark is as miserable as always. The workload he sets is unattainable unless I use my magic, but if I use my magic, there's a fifty-fifty chance that he'll be either impressed or pissed. So..." He tilts his head back, catching every last drop of the ale on his outstretched tongue. "What's there to say?"

"Time to get drunk and disappoint everyone?" I joke. The birth of our sisters is truly a worthy cause for celebration. Three beautiful, healthy girls. Three nights filled with fun and frivolity. Yet our parents still have expectations for how Mallrie and I behave. I don't *want* to get on my parents' bad side, but when the bar is so incredibly high, it's impossible to please them. Though stumbling home as the sun was rising this morning probably didn't help.

"Oh, I've already got something planned." The tone of his voice has me apprehensive, especially when his lips twitch like he's trying to hold in a smile.

"Of course you do. That's probably why Avark caned your hand," I say, nodding to the bruised and broken skin. "You were daydreaming up a plan of some sort."

Mallrie claps me on the back, that knowing smile deepening. "What do you say about a spot of swimming?"

"Who have you got in mind?"

Mallrie claps his hand on my shoulder. "Let's grab a bottle or two and I'll show you. They're already waiting for us."

We make our way through the forest to a nearby river—one our father had tossed us in as kids for misbehaving. My jaw tightens every time Mal and I come here, but he's always got someone or something fantastical waiting for us. I've wondered if he's trying to remove the memory of our father tossing us in here in the middle of winter, replacing it with something more enjoyable. I'd be a fucking liar if I said it wasn't working. Especially when I hear the giggling over the rush of water.

"You get the redhead." Mal winks at me as he places the bottles down on a boulder near the river's edge.

I recognise Ivy the moment I see her red hair piled up on top of her head, a dagger holding it in place. Mallrie didn't have to tell me which woman he had convinced to meet me here. I would have known from the back of her head, and that all too knowing smirk he wore earlier, that he was playing like the Fates, weaving his own little threads, drawing Ivy and I together because I've been too afraid to speak to her myself. A sound I've never heard before rumbles up my throat as I scrub a hand down my face, trying to erase the evidence of the way my lips are curving uncontrollably. I want to equally kiss Mallrie *and* dunk his head under the water and hold him down until he's thrashing, desperate to come up for air.

He knows I have had a little crush on Ivy for months now, ever since she spoke up at training and offered to spar with me. She was quick, ruthless and she didn't seem afraid of me. We hardly spoke as our blades clashed in a dance of death, and I've been trying to get my nerves in order to go up to her and at least *talk* to her ever since.

We quickly strip and join the girls in the water, who instantly move towards us like moths to a flame. Ivy moves towards me, her powerful arms cutting through the strong current before she slips beneath the water. My breath stalls in my throat as she resurfaces right before me, running her hands through the wet tresses of her hair.

She smiles, her green eyes dropping to my lips. "Hi."

My blood rushes hot and my cock hardens at her husky voice, and I struggle to form the simple greeting on my tongue. "He-hey." I grimace to myself, wishing to submerge myself in the river forever.

Ivy chuckles, placing a hand on my shoulder. She moves incredibly close, close enough that I can smell the liquor on her breath as her lips part. The world starts to slip away until it's just the two of—

Ivy pushes herself up using me as she reaches towards the riverbank, retrieving the bottle of wine. My heart stumbles in my chest as her breasts brush against my feverish skin, sending sparks of lightning skittering along my spine. Her nipples are hard little buds, like fresh roses not yet in bloom.

I place my hand on her hip. "Careful," I tell her, as if that's the only reason my hand is so dangerously close to the curve of her ass.

Slipping back into the water, her green eyes find me and her smile has my heart doing a little flip in my chest. "Aren't you just a gem?" she whispers, her legs spreading as she settles down around my hips. "Oh." Her eyes widen with faux shock. "Maybe not as sweet and innocent as you claim to be, Cyan Delacroix."

My hands settle on her hips, forcing her to sit, my erection pressed between us. "I've never claimed to be anything other than what I am."

Her eyes drop to my lips briefly before she looks away, distracting herself with uncorking the bottle of wine. "And what are you?"

She knows exactly what I am. Ivy Bonnay would only be here for one reason. I knew it the moment she reached for that bottle of wine. To piss off her father. If he got wind that she was here with me, he'd be furious.

I hear the whispers in the coven. I know I am the black sheep of our family, the dark stain that people wish they could remove. Mallrie may care and accept me for who I am, but that doesn't mean everyone else does. I'd be a fool to think that Ivy would want to see me again after this. To bring me home to her family. For me to start courting her. She doesn't look at me with that longing, like Cartia is with Mallrie. She's looking at him with such hope, that this might mean more to him than just a quick fuck. It's the way I've looked at Ivy for all these months. Like a fool. Like Cartia.

Mallrie and Ivy are just here for a quick fuck in the dark. A drunken fling to get it out of their systems. And as she slowly grinds her hips against me, something cold settles through me, and I realise I don't mind. Let her use me, cause that infatuation I've felt for months? It's gone, and I'll use her like the whore she is.

CHAPTER NINE

MALLRIE

1841

Summer's unforgiving heat burns onto me as Cyan sits cross-legged, leaning forward intently, listening to the lesson the beautiful earth elemental elder is leading. Sweat dots across my forehead and along the nape of my neck, and yet Cyan looks like he's not even breaking a sweat as he sits there, eyes glistening with interest as he listens to her drawl on and on about some history of... *what was it? Tulips or roses? I can't quite remember.*

Shaking my head, I flick one of the gold metal beads he has intertwined in his long blonde hair. Leaning closer, I whisper, "I don't understand why you wear your hair like this," making sure the other elementals around us don't overhear. Cyan and Father got into a pretty savage fight the other night about Cyan's *lack of direction*, which then resulted in Atherton just yelling about every little thing he despises about him. I love my brother, but there's only so much intervening I can do. Surely, he could at least cut his hair, so it's one less thing they can reprimand him over.

But my stubborn brother just ignores me, waving his hand as if I am nothing more than an annoying fly, buzzing around.

"Mother despises it," I hiss, reminding him what a foul mood our mother tends to get in when the weather warms up. I don't mention our father's distaste for Cyan's choice of hairstyle since he heard it all the other night. Father will tell him to his face exactly what he does that annoys him, whereas Mother tends to just twist her mouth in that disapproving way. She can say more with one look than Father can with an entire yelling fit.

Sometimes I think that's worse.

I look up to the bright blue sky and the fluffy white clouds that don't provide nearly enough shade against the sun. "You don't want to be getting on her bad side this close to the summer festival," I continue, even as he chooses to ignore me.

"Mal, shh!" Cyan's eyes are more green than blue today, but it's still our father's eyes that slide to meet mine. "You'll get us kicked—"

"Mallrie and Cyan Delacroix," the elder snipes, our heads snapping up to where she's standing. Her long, raven black hair is bound in a bubble braid down her back, each section carefully wrapped with the finest golden twine, sparkling in the sunlight.

Multiple heads swivel to where we're sitting at the back of the group. "Is there something the two of you have to share with the rest of the class that is so important?" Her brown eyes fall onto my brother, and his shoulders tense under her scrutiny. "Cyan?"

"No, ma'am." His eyes drop to his boots.

"Sorry, Esmerelda," I smile at the earth elemental I've known since I was a witchling. She's classified as an elder for her skill and knowledge of her magic, however, she's only a few years older than me.

I glance over at Cyan. The tops of his ears are pink with embarrassment, and even though a smile is tugging at the corner of my lips, I feel somewhat guilty for unintentionally drawing the class' attention onto him. He prefers to stay in the shadows, out of the judgemental gazes of others. "It was my fault, I can leave—"

I point a thumb over my shoulder, ready to push myself up from my seated position in the grass, but Esmerelda shakes her head. "No, I think you might learn a thing or two if you stay, Mallrie."

Her pointed stare has me biting back a groan, and Cyan's arrogant smirk makes me want to punch him. Defeated, I fall back onto my ass with a scoff. I know when to keep my mouth shut, unlike Cyan. If I defy Esmerelda, she will go to Mother or Avark and tell them of my disrespect, and I don't want to befall the wrath of either of them.

Elemental lessons are open to anyone of any age or skill, so I've got no leg to stand on with an excuse to leave. Leaning back on my elbows, I can think of a hundred better things I could be doing with my time. Or *who* I could be doing.

Esmerelda claps her hands together, trying to draw everyone's attention back. The witchlings at the front have already broken off into their own conversations, making it more difficult for her to wrangle their attention.

"Thanks a lot," Cyan grumbles through the side of his mouth.

I roll my eyes. "Well, if you didn't drag me along, we could have been doing something more fun."

"Esmerelda is right. You might learn something... like compassion."

I snort and catch the glare of the elder once again. Leaning close to Cyan's ear, I whisper, "I have spades of compassion, brother." Pulling back, I let Esmerelda's dull words about the Language of Flowers flow over me once more. I try to heed her advice, but I find my mind wandering to flashes of dark, soft flesh, lips and hands wrapping around my cock, my hand gripped in long, dark hair...

Someone clears their throat and I look up at Esmerelda, who flicks her black hair over her shoulder, her eyes simmering with displeasure. Between the white dress and gold accents complimenting her dark skin, she looks like some sort of elemental goddess. She glares pointedly in my direction, which I return with a smile. Her cheeks glow a soft pink as she shifts her attention away. Even though what she is talking about is frightfully dull, her eyes sparkle with passion.

The witchlings sitting at the front fidget with the grass, some even practising growing little buds of pink flowers. The field is beautiful and only a few feet within the forest, north of the coven. Positioned at a safe distance away, it offers the perfect place for witchlings to explore on their own without the risk of venturing too far into the forest. It also provides seclusion that shields from the commotion of the coven, allowing lessons to be performed without distraction.

The sun breaks through the trees, washing the wild-flowers of every colour in a golden glow, the gentle breeze catching their scent and gently perfuming the air. I strain to hear the distant clang of metal of the training grounds further east, but their comforting sounds are indistinguishable this far away.

My eyelids grow heavy against the bright sunlight as I

rest my head against my hand, Esmerelda's voice fading into the darkness.

Cyan shakes me awake. I must have dozed off and missed the end of the lesson. *Good riddance*, I think as Esmerelda's simmering gaze lands on me as she talks to one of the witchlings. Apparently, my nap wasn't appreciated by all.

I rub my eyes as Cyan hauls me to my feet. "Did you really fall asleep?" He's talking quickly and animatedly as we walk out of the clearing and back towards the coven. So few people see this side of him, which is a shame. Past the rough and tough exterior Cyan tries to put up, he is kind, generous and... passionate. Sometimes to the point where I am ready to rip my ears off. "How could you have fallen asleep?" He grabs my elbow, pulling me to a sudden stop and giving me a stern look that is purely Atherton Delacroix (not that I'd ever mention that to him).

It's cute, really. He puts on this tough exterior to protect himself from those around him. There's not a doubt in my mind that he's heard the coven discuss him from time to time. I guess he feels that if they won't love him, they may as well fear him. Which seems to work, as some of the other elementals leaving the clearing notice his body language and give us a wide berth. But Cyan will always be my baby brother. Even if some wish he weren't.

"You know," he starts, his tone dripping with smug arrogance, "Mother won't be impressed when she finds out you were disrespectful and fell asleep on Esmerelda."

I wave a hand in the air dismissively, unconcerned with

his attempts to shame me. She won't care if I fell asleep. I know I am our mother's favourite child. *Well, not including our sisters.* But everyone in the coven has a soft spot for those three troublemakers, considering triplets are extremely rare—especially when they're all identical, a symbol of harmony, wisdom and understanding.

Even if she found out, and on the off chance that she got upset, I can always just spin some bullshit that I was up late, practising my magic or deciphering some time elemental scripture. Fates know Avark is always adding another one to the never-ending list. I smile. *It wouldn't be a complete lie. I was up late last night with Briar, or was it Laurel? I guess it doesn't matter—taking a midnight swim in the river. Laurel—or Briar—was concerned that the enchantment in Vaasis mightn't stretch as far as the river. That concern melted away as soon as we slipped into the water.* Memories of her pale skin glistening in the moonlight invade my mind, threatening to make this moment very awkward.

Cyan doesn't seem to notice that I am not listening to him, or that the memory of swimming and fucking what-ever the earth elemental's name was has me needing to readjust myself.

He is talking animatedly about some legend about two lovers who longed to be together, but society forbade their love. I roll my eyes.

"Ferhad heard Shirin had taken her life," Cyan continues, completely oblivious to my lack of attention, "so he killed himself to be with her for eternity." He sighs dramatically. "Tulips grew where his blood spilled—a symbol of his love and devotion." He studies the palm of his hand as a small red tulip appears. "Could you ever imagine loving someone so much, knowing you'd never be together? Then they died before you could even confess your love?" His eyes widen at the thought, as if it would be the worst thing in the world. He, of all people, should know there are worse fates.

I pluck the flower out of his hand, twisting it between my fingers, "Brother," I say, flicking the bud into a nearby bush, "don't bother yourself with such drivel. I'm sure you're not destined for some great love tragedy."

You've fucked enough women that I'm surprised this even bothers you, I think, but don't speak aloud. *Fates, Cyan's even been sneaking off to see a mer! Now, if Mother ever found out about that...*

Cyan looks back at the bush I tossed his silly flower in. The red petals stand out against the lush green foliage like a splatter of blood. I drape an arm across his shoulders, noticing him wince a little. My brows furrow as I see the aggravated piece of skin poking out of his cotton shirt.

I shake my head. I don't understand why he goes through the torment of tattooing his skin. But I don't voice that either. There are some battles I don't bother fighting Cyan over, like his choice of hairstyle or brandishing his skin with ink.

"Why trouble yourself with something unlikely to happen?" I clap my hand on his chest, secretly hoping to hit another sore spot. As much as I love my little brother, I love to rile him up too. "Come, let's go train. I could do with a wake-up after that boring lesson."

CHAPTER TEN

MALLRIE

"Mallrie! What a surprise!" The sound of half a dozen Enkantians' training breaks off at Father's announcement of our arrival. "I didn't expect to see you today."

Cyan bristles at my side with all the attention on us.

"I needed something to wake me up a bit before my lessons this evening with Avark," I say with a laugh, lightening my words as I clap Cyan on the back, his shoulders relaxing under my hand.

"Of course, of course," Atherton says absent-mindedly, his eyes falling to Cyan. "And what are *you* doing here?"

My magic flares under my skin, warning me of the stupidity that's about to come out of Cyan's mouth. The sound of clashing metal echoing off the rocks and trees surrounding us seems to dull into the background.

"Oh, you know, just the usual," he says with an air of casual arrogance as he looks at his nails. "Making you question every choice you've ever made, be a stain of embarrassment on the Delacroix name... take your pick."

Atherton's teeth grind together at Cyan's words, but I

step between the two of them before he can speak. "We won't disrupt anything. We're just here for a little sparring. You'll hardly notice we're here."

"Like that's possible," Atherton snorts, yet the corners of his lips curve slightly. I know he likes to show me off when I come to train. Time elementals are rare, and Avark is too old to fight—or refuses to—so Father likes to showcase my magic in the ring.

I guide Cyan away from Father's not-so-silent seething into the training ring we've claimed as our own, the farthest away from where everyone else prefers to train. Two sides of the ring back onto the rocky cliff that surrounds this area. My gaze finds the small carvings in the rock from when Cyan was a child and he'd sit and watch me practise.

"You ready?" I ask, drawing my long sword, the scrape of the metal like the call of a friend.

"Fuck yeah!" he says, unsheathing his own blade.

From the corner of my eye, I notice Leander taking a seat on a nearby boulder, resting his arms on his knees. Father's boots are the other thing I notice, crunching against the gravel, pacing a safe distance away, as if he's not interested in whatever it is we're doing. But then his voice calls, "No magic. I want to see what you've learnt." Then his voice drops, and it's barely audible over the sounds of metal and grunts, "If anything." And I know he's going to be critiquing Cyan's skills.

The sound of our swords striking against one another echoes off the rocks and trees surrounding us. Stepping forward, I drive my weapon up. The strike vibrates down my arms as my muscles tense against Cyan's force. I focus on my breathing, on the rock sliding beneath my boots as I inch myself forward, forcing him back towards the large boulders.

Our father watches on.

Cyan's eyes widen slightly as the realisation sinks in that I am slowly backing him into a corner. Every ounce of control and strength is evident in the tautness of his muscles and the lock of his jaw.

"No magic, Cyan!" Atherton growls, practically spitting his name like poison in his mouth.

I can feel my magic swelling under my skin, desperate to be unleashed, but there's no doubt in my mind that Cyan has a better hold on his. He always has—he's always had to. Besides, he may fight dirty, but he's no cheat. Even if Father knows this too, he's not afraid to show how deep his distaste for his youngest son runs.

Cyan's knuckles are bleached white, the veins in his wrist turning a deep shade of green. This is why people treat him differently. His magic, unlike that of other earth elementals, often behaves in unpredictable ways, which can intimidate those who prefer stability and predictability. Atherton, for example, holds the belief that change and differences are dangerous, and should be handled with an iron fist. Yet, no matter how many times I warn Cyan to just stay quiet, to hold his bloody tongue, he's too damn stubborn. I think it's remarkable how his body reacts to the world around him. He is truly remarkable, and I wish others could see that instead of their blind fear of what they don't understand. His magic is a gift from the Fates.

A smile stretches across my face as I know I can have Cyan pinned in two—

He lunges, swinging his sword enough that I take a small step back. It's enough for him to jump and roll out of the way, and he pops up like a fucking daisy in the snow behind me, swinging a leg and connecting with my side. He continues his assault with speed and precision that make me believe he was holding me off enough in the hopes that I'd drop my guard.

Something hard knocks against the back of my heel, and I bite back the bark of laughter trying to escape as Cyan continues to push me back against the rocks.

Sword at my throat, I chuckle darkly and drop my weapon. "Good work, little brother." We embrace, our hands clapping together before I turn and pick up two small stones by the wall. "You finally got another mark against your name," I say as I carve another mark under the crudely written *C*.

Cyan laughs. "I believe I should have another one there..."

"No, *no*," I say, trying not to laugh as well. "That time doesn't count. I slipped on the ice."

"Doesn't matter!" Cyan bursts, leaning over my shoulder, trying to take the stones from my hand to add another mark. "If it was war and there *was* ice, you'd be dead!"

"We weren't even supposed to be out here!" I exclaim in a hushed tone, rolling my shoulder and toppling him to the ground. "It was unofficial!"

"It still counts—"

Cyan's laughter fades at the sound of a pair of boots approaching. We both scramble to our feet as our father strides over to where we stand, panting. The joy and humour dissolve like the first fall of snow on a still-too-warm day. I can sense Cyan's body tensing up, readying for the storm that's about to come. Atherton snatches his sword from where it was discarded on the ground, swinging his empty hand. The sound of the impact on Cyan's face has my muscles pulling taut. My magic is pulsing loudly in my ears, and a purple haze blurs at the corners of my vision. To Cyan's credit, he doesn't show any sign of pain even though his cheek is bright red and there's a trickle of blood on the corner of his mouth from the impact.

I steel myself. I don't approve of how our parents treat Cyan, but it's not my place to say anything, lest I want to receive the same punishment.

We've been down that road before. The memory of that terrifying night floods my mind with echoes of raised voices, tense muscles and the biting chill of frigid water.

Cyan's older now. I'd like to think he's learnt some tact in these situations, so he can take care of himself, though I will always feel responsible for him. I am committed to doing everything in my power to keep him out of harm's way.

Cyan lifts a hand to his bloody lip, refraining from snarling back in our father's face. *Keep it together, Cyan*, I silently urge.

"Do you know why I did that?" Atherton grits out between clenched teeth like it's a burden having to explain these things to him.

Cyan diverts his gaze, not answering.

Wrong move, brother.

Atherton's hand snaps out, gripping Cyan's long hair and pulling it taut. The blade glistens in the sunlight as he lifts it above his head. I can't drag my eyes away, my heart pounding in my ears like a ritualising drum reaching its crescendo. The sword falls and my hands ball into fists with restraint to stop my magic from being unleashed. Cyan's hair falls to the ground. "You showed weakness," Atherton snarls.

He really didn't. Yes, the slight widening of his eyes was a tell. But it wasn't something that warranted that overreaction. Father has always been one to act without thoughts of his consequences—especially when it comes to Cyan.

They're in a silent battle. Neither one wants to speak to the other. Both wish the worst. If looks could kill, they'd both be keeling over, taking their last breaths.

Cyan squares his shoulders. "Did I *flinch, Father?*" He spits the word with just as much venom as Atherton did with his name before storming into the Melsheim Forest, not waiting to be dismissed.

Leander has moved away, and Fates bless him, he's trying to draw the attention of the other Enkantians away from us. Atherton won't take his leaving without being dismissed lightly. I watch as Cyan drags a hand over the nape of his neck. My chest constricts at the thought of what he is about to do, and I move to follow him. I can deal with damage control later.

"You encourage him too much," Father says, his hand against my chest to stop me from following my brother.

"I give credit where credit is due," I reply, snapping my shoulders back and raising my chin. Father snorts and mumbles under his breath as he storms off in the opposite direction.

I am left standing in the training ring, my fists clenched at my sides and my gaze fixed on the spot where Cyan vanished into the trees. *I'm finding it harder and harder to find the right words to say to him to ease the tension.*

CHAPTER ELEVEN

CYAN

My anger is like a palpable force around me. As my fingers curl around the straggled strands of hair that survived my father's attack, it ripples through my body and into the earth. It shouldn't bother me as much as it does; it's just hair, after all. It will grow back. But it's *my* body. No one gets to say what I do to it but *me!*

As I storm past, a branch practically jumps out of my way, my hand barely grazing its foliage. I don't need to focus on where I am going. I've walked this path more times than I can count, deeper than we're permitted to go —than any Enkantian *dares* to go. If I strain my ears, I might hear the lorkreigs' furthermost camps. Even I don't have enough of a death wish to venture too close to their camps.

I will kill him. The dark, intrusive thought resurfaces once more, the words reverberating through my skull as the trees blur into a wall of green as I head towards the one place where I can find peace and solitude. *Nothing I ever do will be good enough for him.* Anger and sadness are at war with each other in my chest until I am struggling to breathe. I've tried *everything* to make him proud of me. I've cut my hair the same as Mallrie, wearing the same clothes and doing the same things. I've cut and moulded myself to be a reflection of my brother, even if it made me feel sick to do so, but it was *never* fucking good enough!

He's training us to be killers, which will be his downfall.

The crudely chopped hair brushes against my fingers, and something deep within my chest aches at the feel. As I approach the clearing, the thick trees start to thin out, and the ground beneath my bare feet becomes progressively softer. I toss my boots aside, just like my family does me. I reach behind my head, the short strands of my hair brushing against my wrist as I pull my shirt over my head angrily. The soil turns muddy, and I watch as the mud between my toes melts away in the lake's crystal clear waters, like cleaning away blood after a fight.

The chilly water climbs over my knees and I dive, sucking in a final lungful of air before it engulfs me like a thousand tiny needles pricking at my skin. My heart pounds loudly in my ears as I swim down, adrenaline coursing through my veins, reminding me that I am alive.

Tiny bubbles escape from my lips as I reach the bottom, my nails cutting against the sharp river rocks. I watch the watery ribbons of blood dissolve as my body convulses, desperate for air. My lungs burn, and I wonder if I should just take a deep breath. Allow the water to consume my body and soul. Let my body rot down here for the mer to feast upon.

It would be of no loss to the coven.

I doubt anyone would even notice if I was gone.

But I know that to be a partially empty lie. Mallrie would notice.

My entire chest feels on fire; my body screams to swim

to the surface, but I stubbornly dig my hands into the rocky soil, fighting against my body's natural reaction to save itself. I look up at the shimmering water that surrounds me.

There's nothing left for me up there.

The weight on my chest is unbearable. My mind and body are fighting against each other. The rock I'm clutching cuts into my hands, my nails splitting with how tightly I'm holding on. I breathe out the last of my oxygen and watch the bubbles float free, chasing the sunlight. My body spasms again, and my throat feels like it's closing up. Involuntarily, I take a deep breath in. My mind screams at my body to breathe, but all I get is a lungful of water.

It'll be better this way. Mallrie won't have to defend me. Our sisters will forget me. It'll all be over soon.

Pain skitters up my fingers as my nails crack as I fight against the urge to swim to the surface. Squeezing my eyes shut, I try to block out the burning in my chest, the pounding in my head.

It'll all be over soon.

The water stuck in my throat tastes like dirt and death. Something grabs me under the arms, propelling me towards the surface.

As my back hits the ground, the blinding sun burns my eyes, and a gurgle of water spews from my lips. I struggle to roll onto my side.

What the fuck?

My body jerks and shudders as I struggle to spit up the lake water and simultaneously breathe precious air back into my lungs. The sun burns my eyes, and my lungs feel like I have swallowed fire as a hand punches against my back, causing more water to spew up.

"Stupid witch!" curses the mermaid as she flips me onto my back. For a feared predator, she looks like an angel. Her long blonde hair hooks over a delicate fin-like ear, her skin sparkling in the light. A bubble of laughter erupts from my chest as she slaps my hand away from her ear. Mermaids' ears are extremely sensitive.

"Fuck, I love your ears." The delirious thought slips between my lips, but there's no hint of a reprieve in Azalea's stony expression.

"What the fuck do you think you're doing, Cyan?" A webbed hand swats at my chest, hitting that particularly sensitive spot near my shoulder that the rose and serpent tattoo covers.

"You could have drowned! You were drowning!" Her sweet siren's voice is an incensed shrill, breaking through my thoughts as she continues to pound against my chest, no longer trying to help me, but out of vexation.

"Would that have been so bad, Az?" I rasp, the words burning my throat. "I know how much you like to feast on me. Why not do it for good?"

Azalea pushes herself into a sitting position and props a webbed hand against her hip, where her human body morphs into a beautiful, olive green-golden ombre tail. Her stony stare softens and a sultry smile spreads across her face. "Why do it for good when, like you pointed out, you're already enough of a snack?" she purrs. Her eyes are hooded with lust as they gaze down my torso where my tunic is clinging to the contours of my body.

"Oh, please, I'm a whole damn meal!" I scoff, pushing myself up onto my elbows and glaring at her. "The best fuck you've had in a *long* time."

Azalea hums sweetly. "Then why were you trying to kill yourself? Why deny me the best sex *either* of us has ever had?"

I flop back onto the grassy bank. "Why not?"

"Your parents are just... threatened by you." Az chooses her words carefully, her fingers tracing around the tattoos I have to cover some of Atherton's wounds. The mer are mysterious creatures, and I know Azalea knows *something*.

When I first met her, she wasn't what I was expecting. She was nothing like the man-eating sirens who lure men into the water, where they have their way with them before devouring their bodies. But she was... curious. Curious why I was sitting on a rock crying, cradling a broken wrist, the result of the only time Atherton trained with me one-on-one.

Azalea asked me a lot of questions that day, and the next, after asking me to return. Soon, I found that whenever things in the coven felt like they were too much, I'd escape to this place. A place many would keep away from because of the dangers that surrounded it, but it was a place where I felt seen and heard.

The merfolk are perplexing creatures. Whenever I question Az, she always deflects, or her answers are vague. So, I am used to not getting any answers from her.

"I'm going to kill him," I grit out between my teeth, finally sitting up and resting my arms on my bent knees as I stare at the shimmering water. The thought burns through my mind with such a force that I don't hear what Az is saying. It's a familiar one. A recurring fantasy that's played in my mind countless nights, going over what would happen if I ever got the balls to do it.

From the corner of my eye, I see her tilt her pretty head as if waiting for my reply. She's more than just a good fuck. Not that I'd admit it to her. Some days, I feel like Azalea is my only friend.

Her webbed fingers run through my short hair, sending a shiver down my spine. "Because your father cut your hair again?" she whispers, as if afraid the trees will hear her. I don't know why it bothers me; it's just hair. It'll grow back. Az shimmies her body closer to mine, as if sensing where my thoughts have gone. "You know, some people are very protective about their hair—"

"Don't you fucking compare me to a lorkreig again." I glare at her and she shifts away from me. She may be a predator in the water, but sitting on the bank beside me, she's *my* prey.

I enjoy how she cowers away from me, diverting her eyes down to her tail, watching her fins float in the water, catching and reflecting the sunlight. Azalea hums innocently. "Sorry," she sings as she flicks a lock of her hair over her shoulder, exposing her breast and the jewellery I pierced through those rosebud nipples many moons ago. "But you realise, we mer also hold our hair in high regard, too," she adds, flicking the other side and tilting her head back, showing off her perfect tits.

"Yeah, to lure stupid men to their death," I drawl, unable to take my eyes off her breasts, from the droplets racing over their swells to the way her nipples harden when the air caresses them.

Az waves her hand, snapping me out of my trance. "See? You're all the same. We all are, you know?"

"Ah, fuck, here we go," I groan, falling back on the bank, covering my eyes.

"I'm serious," Az giggles, moving closer and tugging my arm free. "I don't understand why some think that they're better than others."

I wrap my arm around her waist, pulling her closer. "Maybe because they're told that the merfolk only want one thing." I wink.

Azalea laughs again, and it's such a beautiful sound. "I've heard the same about young witches."

"Well, you're not wrong there," I snort.

She smiles at me again, and I feel like she sees me more than Mallrie ever has. Sometimes I feel that his love is one out of obligation, but Az... she owes me nothing, and I can utterly be myself around her. She sees all the sharp, fucked up, broken pieces of me and loves them irrevocably.

"We're all just creatures trying to live out our lives. Why is one of us any better than the other? We're all intelligent, are we not?"

I run my hand up her tail, causing her to shudder and shift. The scales of her tail shimmer in the light to expose two very *humanoid* legs. I roughly tug them apart. "Yes, Az," I murmur as I lean over and start kissing the inside of her thigh, desperate for a distraction and for her to shut the fuck up. "Whatever you say."

CHAPTER TWELVE
MALLRIE

I know I have to go after Cyan. I swear, when he gets irate like this, all rational thoughts leak from his brain. I worry about what he'll do. But I had to deal with our father first.

The sun is setting dangerously low to be this far in the Melsheim Forest, but the small, green Cyan-shaped flame keeps stalking forward. My magic guides me to him. I roll my eyes as I raise my hand, rolling my wrist, recalling my magic, and then crushing the green flame in my fist as I see a figure stalking through the bush. My muscles go taut as I reach for my weapon, but then I see him. I should have known he'd go to see *her*.

Despite my warnings, Cyan reassures me that the mer —Azalea, as if knowing her name will bring comfort in knowing *what* he is hanging out with—means him no harm.

I shake my head, a rough laugh clawing at my throat that I try to swallow as Cyan emerges, swinging a hand through the flora, water still clinging to the crudely chopped hair. His pants are clinging to his legs, as if he forgot to remove them before he dived dick first into mermaid-infested waters.

"Have a pleasant swim?" I say as a way of greeting, grinning like the cat who caught the mouse. Cyan just keeps walking as if I am not even there. But it's the irritated tattoo on his shoulder that has me grabbing his arm and turning him to face me. "What the fuck is *that?*" I growl. Fear and anger press tightly into my chest until I am struggling to breathe.

Cyan follows my line of sight before his eyes snap back up to mine. I can practically see a wall forming around them. "I didn't take you to be dense enough not to notice a tattoo when you see one, *Mallrie.*"

He says my name with such distaste that it has me shifting my weight, readying myself for a fight. My fingers tighten around his arm as I look closer. Under the irritation and black ink... there's a scar.

It appears to be healed *so* well that I wonder if he sought the herb Avark enchants to speed up healing because I know every scar on Cyan's body, given I have been the only person in his life who cares enough to notice, and I do not recognise this one.

"What happened?" My fingers dig deeper into his flesh and his eyes flash to where I'm gripping him. *Whoever laid a finger on my brother, whoever hurt him...* "Cyan—"

"*Father,*" he interrupts, and my body stills. "Thought it best to give me some... additional training."

My blood turns to ice, my greatest fear flashing before my eyes. "You weren't training, were you?" I say, closing my eyes and trying to steady my breathing. My fucking chest feels like it's being ripped open as the words sit heavily on my tongue, leaving a foul taste behind.

Cyan scoffs. "*I* was training. Minding my own business

when *he* threw a dagger at me!" He pushes himself out of my grip. "Bastard sauntered over, ripped out the blade and muttered" —Cyan leans in, a dark, murderous glint in his eyes— *"missed."*

"Fuck. Cyan..." I breathe, and his eyes trail down my body, looking for something. His gaze stills on the dagger strapped to my thigh. He snatches it out of its sheath and tosses his shirt and boots into my arms before stalking back through the forest towards the coven. "Fuck!" I hiss. I know that look in his eyes. "Cyan, come back!"

The forest bends at his will, making it harder for me to chase him. The earth rumbles under my feet, shaking almost violently as boulders appear out of the ground, blocking my way. Trees that have stood for millennia creak and crack until they're falling in my path.

"Cyan!" I shout. My fingers brush his shoulder, yet he slips through, barely glancing over his shoulder at me. Roots and vines claw at my boots, trying to slow me down, but I allow a kernel of my magic to seep away, slowing their progress and Cyan's steps until I am finally standing before him. My hands gripping his shoulders to cease his incessant, murderous march.

"What do you think you're going to do? Kill him?" I ask, breathing heavily at the idea. It's utterly absurd. Cyan has spoken about murdering Atherton from time to time, but has never been entirely sold on the idea of taking a life.

He swings the blade, and the metallic taste of blood floods my mouth. I fall to my knees, pressing a hand to my face. Hot and sticky blood pours over my hands, dripping onto my pants and the leaves as I pant, trying to breathe through the searing pain.

I look up at Cyan standing before me, the bloody dagger in hand. "That's *exactly* what I am going to do," he growls, his eyes black with rage, "and I suggest you keep out of my fucking way."

I can't let him do something he will regret.

"Cyan... wait..." the words come out slurred as I push to my feet. Part of my mouth feels numb with the pain and... *floppy*. I swallow the bile climbing up my throat and my magic pulses through my veins, racing towards the wound to slow the bleeding. Snapping my hand out, I grab him by the wrist that holds the dagger. I squeeze tightly, trying to hit that pressure point that will have his hand splaying wide, releasing the weapon.

Cyan swings his leg, catching me behind my knee. I fall hard onto my back, the wind knocked from my lungs. He is on top of me before I can move, vines ripping from the ground, holding me down. It feels like the earth is ready to swallow me whole, squeezing all the oxygen out of me. "Brother..." I plead as a vine wraps around my throat.

"If I don't kill him, he'll kill me, Mallrie. You know that, don't you?" Tears prick at his eyes, and my heart cracks open.

He's right. It's not the first time Atherton has tried to kill him, and it won't be the last.

I don't reply. How can I?

"I am not the bad guy here, Mallrie." Cyan's voice cracks, and seeing him before me like this rips my heart in two. His words land like a physical blow to the chest. "I am the fuck up. The child no one wanted. You get *everything*." He looks at me, not with disdain or loathing, but... *longing*. "I have a family who doesn't care if I live or die. I'm dead but never mourned."

Tears prick at my eyes as I shake my head. I have tried to love him enough for our family, but it's not enough. *I* am not enough.

Cyan's eyes narrow. "What aren't you telling me?"

My brows press together. "Nothing," I breathe, a weight of a thousand unsaid words heavy on my tongue. "You're my brother, and I love you. I don't want you to do something that you'll regret."

Cyan blinks away the tears. I think I am the first person who's ever told him they love him. I am not one for words of affection, but I mean it, and he needs to hear it. But I think I also need to say it aloud for myself, so I say it again.

"You're my brother, Cyan. I love you."

CHAPTER THIRTEEN

CYAN

"What did you just say?" Mallrie's words have me dazed, and for a moment, I feel like I've forgotten how to breathe.

"Don't do this, Cyan. You don't need that blood on your hands. I-I'll figure this out, I promise."

"No," I breathe. "Not that."

Mallrie's face pinches with confusion as he tries to recall what he said before trying to convince me not to murder Atherton. Despite Azalea talking to me about the consequences of murdering my father, my mind is made up. If I am honest with myself, it's been made up for quite some time.

The vines that were wrapping around Mallrie and pinning him to the ground have fallen loose. I take a step back, as if putting distance between us will force those three little words back down his throat.

"Cyan, you're my brother," Mallrie says with a hint of disbelief, getting to his feet. "I love you."

There it is. My back teeth grind at the words.

Mallrie takes a step closer. "You are my flesh and blood.

You and our sisters are my entire world." His gaze shudders as he looks away, his voice dropping to a whisper. "Mother calls me selfish. I should treat everyone equally in the coven... but I can't. You, Alinta, Riri and Abeline are too important to me."

My hands shake. The weight of the dagger in my hand is too much. I look at Mallrie's bloody face, his lip trying to pull itself back together. Bile climbs up my throat at the grotesque sight of him. Of what *I* did to him.

"You don't have to do this, Cyan." Mallrie's voice is gentle as his hand wraps around mine, sliding the dagger out of my grip. "I will figure something—"

"NO!" My teeth grind together as I straighten myself. "I *have* to do this, Mallrie. It ends now. I won't involve you in this. You've done too much already."

Mallrie steps back, and I can see the regret in his eyes. "No. I haven't." His voice cracks with the words.

I cannot look at him. He looks so much like our father, it hurts sometimes. My bottom lip wobbles as I whisper, finally speaking what's been on my mind for years. "Why doesn't he love me?" My fingers graze over my hair as I aggressively swipe at my cheeks. "I've tried so hard." Mallrie's arms are around me in an instant, and my knees buckle in his embrace. "What did I do wrong?"

"I don't know." He chews on his lip like he's trying to find the right words. "I remember the first time I saw him raise a hand at you." His voice is barely above a whisper, but I can hear the tremble in it. "It was one of the few times I slowed *Time*. Avark had given me a stern lecture that day about manipulating it. Still, I couldn't remember a word of it when Atherton raised a hand at you." Mallrie's eyes meet mine. "You were two, crying because you couldn't get your mind and tongue to work in tandem to speak what you needed." I can almost feel him shaking with anger.

An image makes its way into my mind, a memory. A small, blonde-haired boy screaming and crying, and then our father's face, red with rage as he lifts his hand. Everything moves incredibly slow, or I am just moving exceptionally fast.

No, it's not me.

It's Mallrie.

His body takes the blow, and the memory blurs momentarily as darkness seeps into my vision's corners. I don't know if the memory wants to fade out or if Father struck him so hard that he almost blacked out.

Either way, a wave of appreciation washes over me. *If Mallrie didn't intercept that attack...*

I shudder at the thought of what damage could have happened to a child that small. To *me*.

In the memory, Mallrie is shouting at our father, and then his hands are wrapping around that small blonde boy's tiny body, lifting me into his arms. I've stopped screaming, but tears silently stream down my small face like rivers. Mallrie's arms tighten around my tiny body. Lifting his chin, he sneers, "Don't you *dare* raise your hand to my brother again. He is *your* flesh and blood, Father. You best remember that." Mallrie turns his attention back to the small boy in his arms.

Blinking, that small boy, his blonde hair and dark green eyes bright with tears, fades out and morphs back into my brother before me. Mallrie looks shocked. "I'm sorry," he breathes. "I-I didn't mean to show you that."

"You protected me?"

He nods gravely. "I always have. When I could. I'm sorry I haven't been doing a very good job." His voice is distant, filled with regrets and burdens that no child should ever have to carry.

"Thank you," I whisper, still unable to meet his eyes. Even though Mallrie has never looked at me with hate—and he isn't now—all I can see is our father's hateful glare. "But I am still going to murder him."

Mallrie steps back, nodding his head and stepping past me. He picks up the dagger. Turning to face me, he looks at the blood-stained blade in his hand. It was a gift to him from our father for his eighteenth birthday. Father made a big song and dance about getting it specifically forged for Mallrie.

When I turned eighteen, I got nothing.

"I understand," is all Mallrie says as he wipes the blood from the dagger on his pants, leaving a dark smear across his knee. His voice is like the coldest winter, and I wonder if he's going to stop me. Instead, he closes his eyes, his lips moving silently as he places his hand over the blade, running the edge through his clenched fist. I step forward, a gasp and a protest on my lips, but Mallrie snaps his eyes open. There is a soft, purple glow there, and whatever protest I had dies on my tongue as I watch his magic become a tangible thing of purple smoke, filled with little stars and constellations.

Time. A gift from the Fates.

Mallrie's magic twists around his hand and the dagger before being absorbed by the dark metal. Then the light is gone from his eyes and transferred to the blade in his hand. He holds the glowing weapon out to me.

"Wh-what did you do to it?" I breathe, taking the dagger from him and turning it, examining the blade. I've never feared Mallrie or his magic, despite it being as mysterious as the Fates themselves. Avark takes him away from the coven to practise his magic. No one truly knows what they're doing in that cave. *Mallrie would never hurt me*, I remind myself, but there's something dark and unnatural about this that has my skin crawling. Something deep inside me is screaming to destroy the blade.

"Something I shouldn't have," he utters, shame and anger colouring his cheeks. "But a parent should never hurt their child like Father has you."

Emotion clogs my throat as I finally look Mallrie in the eye again.

"Be warned, brother, that blade is now lethal and should only be wielded with a sound mind. Whoever is slain by that blade will forever be entwined in it."

I think my eyebrows must fly off the top of my head as a single word pushes out all the oxygen in my body. *"What?"* I exclaim. *I don't understand how this is possible.*

Why, this is—

How Mallrie—

My thoughts are a scrambled mess, one constantly overpowering the other, and I am left standing there, blinking and gaping at Mallrie like a fish out of water.

"Atherton Delacroix will not know peace. You keep the blade and never use it again, or destroy it. Either way, Atherton's soul shall never enter Vraska and the Afterlife."

CHAPTER FOURTEEN
CYAN

The sun is falling deeper behind the trees, plunging the forest into darkness. My fingers tighten around the dagger. We're too far away from the coven, from the protection Vaasis offers, but all I can think about is what Mallrie has done, what he has offered me. Not only his aid and his dagger but also his magic.

"What's your plan? Because if the High Witchess catches you, she'll have you burnt," Mallrie warns, his words calculated and distant. I don't miss the fact that he referred to our mother by her title.

Unease burns in my gut as I shift uncomfortably on my feet at his tone—one I've rarely heard before. "I-I hadn't..." In my anger, I hadn't thought about what I'll do. Embarrassment colours my cheeks as I look away, trying to quickly come up with some plan that doesn't result in my death or make Atherton suspect Mallrie's involvement.

"The girls need to be somewhere safe. That's a non-negotiable," Mallrie murmurs more to himself than to me as his thumb brushes over his lips in contemplation. A small bead of blood catches on the pad of his thumb and his eyes focus on it.

"I agree," I mutter, my senses alert as a stick crunches somewhere in the distance, but Mallrie doesn't look up from his hand.

"Cora and Lia—"

Snap.

My grip tightens on the dagger. Something is watching us. My pulse races through my head. "I'd trust them with my life. I'll ask Cora to watch the girls," Mallrie continues, completely oblivious of whatever is watching us, hunting us.

"Mal..."

"I'll get mother away too. She'll kill us if she finds out what we're planning."

"We?" I look back at my brother, at the serious look on his face. "I've told you, you don't have to do this. I don't need your help."

"And I've told you before—" An obscene string of curses cut Mallrie's words off. "*Down!*" he growls, pushing me onto my knees and swinging his leg over my head, a fleshy *thwack* sounding instantaneously. Turning, I find a tall creature with brownish, leathery skin pressed tightly against its bones. Long sword-like arms flail as it stumbles backwards.

Magic courses through my body and then roots explode through the dirt, spearing the Kailadon in the chest and head, killing the beast.

Mallrie eyes the creature as the roots pull it back down to the earth, its lifeless face pressed open in a silent scream. "I've told you, Cyan, you don't have to do this alone."

I know there will be no talking him out of this. "Thank you." The words choke on the rock forming in my throat.

Mallrie points to the Kailadon still being crushed by the roots. "You need to be like that when the time comes. You'll only get one chance."

I try to swallow, but it feels almost impossible, like my throat is closing in on itself. I can't do anything but nod.

"You're a good man, Cyan. Murder will fracture your soul. That" —Mallrie points again at the Kailadon— "doesn't count. That's a matter of life and death. What you're about to do is actively attack and murder one of your own. Atherton is a part of your coven. He's a husband, a father. You have to be prepared to take that life." He scrubs a hand over his face, over the fine dusting of dark hair along his jawline, contemplating his next words. Mallrie is going against everything the High Witchess has trained him for. If he is to become the High Witch in Cersei's footsteps, he needs to swear an oath to never harm another Enkantian, another member of our coven.

"Cyan, he *will* kill you—mercilessly—if you hesitate. My advice?" Mallrie's tongue darts along his lips, as if voicing this advice is taking its toll on him. I wish I could take this burden away from him. "Go find an innocent to kill. I don't care if it's a mouse. Feel its blood on your hands and watch the light leave its eyes, because once you murder in cold blood, you'll never be the same again. Don't take Atherton's death lightly. Death should always be felt. As much of a monster as he is, he is still your flesh and blood, and he has the right to live. As do you."

A silence has fallen across the forest like a blanket as if it knows that Death is here, waiting. Mallrie put an enchantment around the area to protect me from any more wandering Kailadons or any of the other vile creatures that lurk within the Melsheim Forest. The weight of his dagger sits in the palm of my hand, his words in my mind while I wait for something to cross my path. I don't relish the idea of killing an innocent creature, but Mallrie is right. If I don't want a slow and painful death myself, I will need to know what to expect. But, of course, killing a small creature will vastly differ from a fully grown man.

A Nechkrappe lands a few feet before me, scratching at the dirt.

Of course, I think. *With the idea of death hanging so potentially in the air, of course a Nechkrappe would appear.*

The large black bird straightens its spine, swivelling its head around, pinning me with those unsettling white eyes.

An unnerving omen.

If I kill a Nechkrappe, I will either be cursed or know that I have what it takes to kill my father. But time is against us. I need to return to the coven to ensure Mallrie has safely taken the girls to Lia and Cora's, and that Cersei cannot interfere. I didn't ask him how he'd get the High Witchess out of the coven this late, but I've already asked too much of my brother.

Slowly, I lower myself down to my knees so as not to spook the creature. Its eyes narrow slightly, as if trying to figure out what I am doing. The trees shift nervously on a silent breeze. My fingers sink into the earth, and I can feel her calling to me. I can feel the roots shift deep under the soil, the worms wriggling out of the way as my magic reaches into the core.

The Nechkrappe's feathers fluff up and it opens its neb

as if it's about to shriek at me. But before any sound can leave its beak, vines break from the soil and bind the creature, wrapping around its beak, body and legs, slowly squeezing.

"You can't curse me," I whisper matter-of-factly as I approach the Nechkrappe. "I'm already cursed."

The bird has stopped its thrashing and looks at me as if it understands what I am saying, and not just on a basic level. The Nechkrappe narrows its milky eyes at me. We are frozen for a moment, the beast's air slowly being crushed under the vines with me crouched over it, like the Fates with their dead, outstretched hands, waiting to take it to Vraska.

The vines slacken and the Nechkrappe wriggles out of the embrace. I let out an exasperated breath. "Fuck," I curse as the beast flies into a nearby tree, no doubt ready to bestow a curse on me.

The large black bird tilts its head and I brace for whatever dark magic it possesses to wash over me. What I don't expect is to hear a sensual female voice slither into my mind. *"Why did you try to kill me, son of Atherton?"*

My brows pinch together with confusion at the unexpected voice. Looking around, my muscles tense, ready to fight, Mallrie's cursed dagger tightly gripped in my hand. But the forest is empty and eerily quiet. *Is it because of Mallrie's enchantment or because death lingers above me on a branch?* The sound of dry leaves and twigs crunching under my boots is too loud in my ears as that female voice linger in my mind. I stare at Mallrie's dagger before me as my fingers claw into the soft soil. "I didn't want to," I whisper, unable to hide the tremor in my voice, unsure who or *what* I am speaking to. "I just needed practise."

"To kill your father. Tsk tsk tsk. What a son you are!" the

voice scolds, and I hear the distant cawing of the Nechkrappe. My head snaps up to where it's sitting in the tree. A rock forms in my hand, and I toss it at the creature, who caws furiously at me.

Curious. I think. *I thought I'd have felt the Nechkrappe's magic wash over me.*

"What makes you think that, boy?" The enormous bird's voice is soft inside my mind, like crushed velvet, unlike the awful caw I can distantly hear. *"And do not throw another rock at me, or you will feel my wrath!"*

My brows press together. "You can hear my thoughts?" I ask, dumbfounded, unsure why I am still speaking. All our knowledge of these dark, cursed creatures, and we never knew that they could read minds! *This changes everything we thought we knew about them.*

"Yes. And don't think you'll go back, blabbing about it either, will you, boy? Otherwise, I'll pay a visit to your brother and sisters," it hisses. *"And I am a female!"* she shouts into my mind, making me press my hands over my ears.

The female Nechkrappe jumps from the branch she's perched on and lands before me, turning her body this way and that, as if to prove she has a female figure. "Oh, yeah, of *course* you're a girl," I mock, as if it is entirely apparent now.

She sounds like she just clicked her tongue at me, and I can see the dark grey pupils hidden behind the milky exterior roll. *"You didn't answer my question, boy."*

"And I'm not a boy. My name is Cyan. Cyan Delacroix."

"Well, Cyan Delacroix, why are you trying to murder your father, Atherton Delacroix, in cold blood?"

I flinch at her harsh and uncensored words.

"Is that not what you and your brother, Mallrie, are conspiring to do?" she tacks on the end, as if rifling through my thoughts and memories.

"Stay the *fuck* out of my head!" I shout, pressing my hands over my ears. As if that could stop her. The Nechkrappe angles her head, waiting patiently. I drop my head, shame pressing over my skin painfully as I whisper, "Because he wants me dead."

CHAPTER FIFTEEN

MALLRIE

When I see Cora moving about through the window of her modest home and placing a steaming pie on the table, it's like a weight has been lifted from my chest. My fist freezes an inch from the wooden door, my breath stalling in my throat, and I fear I may have slowed time accidentally by the way my body feels unnaturally flushed. But Cora opens the door, her face pinched with concern as she looks at all the blood staining my tunic, dried on my face, neck and hands.

Cora looks around me—since she can no longer just glance over my head—before taking my hand and pulling me inside, locking the door behind us. She's always had more of a maternal intuition than my own mother. Cora has always known when something is wrong and what to say to make it right again. I think that's why I trust her enough to confide in her help tonight.

"I need your help." The words cannot come out of my mouth fast enough, and I feel like that small child once again, coming here and asking her for help to ease Cyan's fever when he was a babe. All these years later, and the same lump sits in the base of my throat, fear and panic pressing against my neck like a restraint. I don't know if leaving Cyan in the forest alone with a cursed blade and this deranged notion to kill Atherton was the right thing to do, but what I do know is that he was right. Atherton will stop at nothing to kill him. It'll look like an accident, of course, and it may not even happen this week or the next. Fates, it could be years from now, but Cyan will never know peace and happiness while Atherton is alive and plotting. And after all, doesn't he deserve that?

Cora guides me into the kitchen and I can smell the sweet scent of apples simmering on the stove. My feet hesitate. Twenty-seven years of age, and I am still terrified to step foot in Cora's kitchen when she's cooking. Even though I now tower over her, I still keep clear when she ties that apron around her waist and wields her wooden spoon.

"Sit down, Mal," she says in that soothing voice that has the nerves in my chest easing a little.

I let her guide me into the kitchen, where she gestures for me to sit on a small stool in the corner that she uses to get ingredients off the tall shelves; the same stool I've sat on in the past when I've come to Cora for help or advice. When I couldn't turn to my own parents. My head falls into my hands as I rest my elbows on my knees.

I shouldn't have left Cyan alone. I should just take care of this myself. He shouldn't have to carry this blood on his hands.

Three words keep ringing in my ears through the maelstrom of thoughts and potential scenarios.

I've failed him.

I've failed him.

I've failed him.

"Mallrie?" Cora gently pulls my hands away from my face and swipes a thumb across my cheek. It comes away damp. "What's happened, sweetie?" Her brows pinch together as her eyes linger on my lip. I can hardly feel my magic stitching up the wound anymore, and I hate to think of Avark's punishment when I see him for using my magic for something so... *selfish.*

Those three words spill from my lips like a virus taking over my body. "I've failed him. Fuck, I've failed him, Cora!" I hate the way my voice cracks, the emotion revealing all my shortcomings.

"Who, sweetie?" Her brown eyes search my face, her hands gently rubbing soothing circles on my back.

"Cyan..." It all but chokes me to get his name out, and I stand to leave. *He shouldn't have to deal with this. It's my fault he's in this situation. I won't let him murder his own father.*

"Oh, Mallrie," Cora says as she steps before me, cupping my face in her scarred hands and angling it down so I am looking at her. "You haven't failed him. You've done your best to raise a child when you yourself were one. That's something you never should have had to do." My jaw aches from trying to hold back the emotion. Atherton would be disgusted with Cyan and me this evening. We've let our emotions run wild. "What can I do to help, Mallrie?" Cora taps my cheek, drawing my attention back to her. She's still so beautiful, her brown eyes filled with kindness. Cyan was always welcome here. Even if Lia was more hesitant about allowing him in their home, Cora always made sure Cyan never went hungry and filled his pockets with sweets, just like she did for me.

I know I can trust her, and I love her as if she were my own mother, but I don't know how even our relationship will withstand what I am about to ask of her. Clearing my throat, I turn her so her back is to the stool. "I think you should take a seat."

Cora's brown eyes shimmer with concern. "Mallrie, you're scaring me." She reaches out again for my face, her fingers brushing against my lips. "What happened?"

I touch the spot on my lip where Cyan sliced the skin in half. "It's nothing. I need your help and... it'd be best if you didn't ask questions."

Cora pushes to her feet, her hands on her hips, a scowl on her face. "Mallrie Elias Delacroix, when have you ever asked me to do something blindly?"

"Never, but—"

"Then you'll know that I won't do it. I love you, Fates damnit, but I won't let you do something reckless and stupid—"

"I need you to watch the girls tonight," I blurt out because she's right. This is reckless and stupid, but if we don't do it... I shudder at the thought of what could happen to Cyan. As if responding to where my thoughts have gone, my magic sings in my blood, trying to draw on those Fate lines to show me what the future holds.

"Oh." Cora doesn't look entirely convinced as she narrows her eyes at me. "Why?"

A slice of pain shoots through me as my teeth graze against the wound, and I take Cora's hands in my own, my thumb stroking across the scarring. "I love you so much, Cora. If I'm honest with myself, you're the mother I wish I had. Both you and Lia. But the Fates didn't bless me with such loving parents, nor did they bless Cyan with them."

Cora shakes her head. "Your parents love you, Mallrie."

"It's not me I'm worried about."

Cora drops her hands, a small *'Ah'* slipping from her lips. Realisation settles across her face. "Both of them?" she asks quietly.

I shake my head. "Just Atherton."

Cora looks at me in bewilderment. I don't sugar-coat the plan I've devised to help Cyan murder Atherton and what my involvement in that will be. I need her help.

"Cora, *please* don't look at me like that." I can't stand it. My heart feels like it's falling from my chest to the floor.

"What you're asking me for is..."

"He *will* kill Cyan, Cora," I say, taking her hand in my own. It trembles slightly and a part of me wants to drop it. To apologise and leave. This is too much to ask of her; to lie to her wife, her coven and her High Witchess. "I know the coven—"

"I know, Mallrie," Cora says, squeezing my hand gently. "I understand." Her eyes turn sympathetic as she tucks a strand of dark brown hair that's becoming lighter with age behind her ear. "Cyan is... something," she starts carefully. "There is no denying that he will be very powerful. His magic makes people apprehensive."

Something inside me twists at her words, at this irrational fear the coven has of Cyan and his differences.

"But I remember a little boy coming to me covered in bruises." She reaches up and touches my face, as if she can still see them. "He swore black and blue that they were from training. But he forgot I married one of the best warriors the Enkantians have. I know the difference between battle bruises and someone taking a beating." I lean into her warm hand, her magic caressing my skin and warming my body. "You love him."

I frown at her, pulling her hand away from my face. "Of course I love him. He's my brother."

She gives me a weak smile. "There are rumours that Cyan—"

"I'd think you are old and wise enough not to listen to

the idle chit-chat of bored housewives, Cora," I growl, my hands balling into fists at my sides.

"You're right," she says, and I know I've struck a nerve. "I apologise, Mallrie." She reaches for my hands again, smoothing out my anger. "I will help you. No child should have to fear for their life. But if the High Witchess finds out it was him, she will burn him for it."

"I know." I also know that as much as I wish I could take this burden from him, my brother is as stubborn as a thistle in one's side. When he's got his mind set on something, it's almost impossible to change it. "That's why I'm helping him."

Cora's eyes glisten with unshed tears. "I'm proud of you, Mallrie. You'll make a wonderful High Witch one day."

CHAPTER SIXTEEN

CYAN

My boots crunch as I wear a path in front of the tree the Nechkrappe sits in, trying to wrap my head around everything that's happened. That's *happening*. Mallrie's dagger glows in the corner of my eye, and I lift it with a shaking hand. The sensual female voice whispers in my ear, invading my thoughts once again. *"I like you, Cyan Delacroix, son of Atherton Delacroix."*

"I don't know why," I whisper. "I tried to kill you."

"Because you were so bold as to try," she replies, and I can almost hear a smile in her voice. *"So I think I will help you."*

My muscles tighten as I whirl to look at the creature. "Why should I trust you? Nechkrappes are notorious tricksters, creatures of destruction and chaos. Nothing good comes about while you're around."

The female gasps loudly in my mind. *"Cyan Delacroix, son of Atherton Delacroix, you wound me!"* Yet I can hear a sense of pride in her voice.

"Stop calling me that!" I shout. Hearing my hateful father's name has my stomach twisting with anger and disgust. "I am no Delacroix."

Again, I can almost hear the smile in her voice as she coos, *"Alright then, just Cyan. Son of no one, born of dishonesties and deceit, of the blood of—"*

"STOP!" I shout, clutching my hands over my ears, as if that'll block out her incessant ramblings. Fates, it's a miracle the Nechkrappes have gone so long with no one knowing that they can speak. This one certainly likes to hear the sound of her own voice. "I am *just* Cyan, the second son of the High Witchess, the one who was never wanted. End. Of. Story."

"Very well. I still wish to help you," she replies. I imagine if she were not a bird, she'd be someone I'd like very much. Despite her ceaseless chatter, she's got a spark that makes me want to smile. I would if Mallrie and I weren't in such a mess.

"Why do you want to help me?" I question. Her willingness to help is making me weary. Mallrie sang bedtime stories warning about Nechkrappes and the evil they possess.

"Were you dropped a lot as a baby?" She sighs. *"I already told you. I like you."*

I eye the black bird as she ruffles her feathers and grooms herself. "What is your name?" I ask. If I am going to get help from a Nechkrappe, I want to at least know her name, so I know who I will need to hunt down if this all turns to shit.

The large black bird twists her head to the point that it almost looks painful. *"I do not have a name."*

"Then what do your friends and family call you?"

Her laughter is harsh and cold in my mind, her caw mimicking the sound. *"What makes you think I have friends or family? I am a Nechkrappe, after all."*

"Surely you have a family? Where did you come from?"

I'm stalling, wasting time because my fear is slowly over-riding my anger. *I couldn't even kill a godsdamned bird. What makes me think I can kill a grown man who's spent most of his days training for a war he might never see?*

"The males impregnate the females and then leave," she says, drawing my attention back to her and the danger that's before me now rather than the danger that awaits me when I return to the coven. *"The females lay the eggs, wait for their babies to hatch and feed them for three weeks until they're strong enough to fend for themselves. Then it is every Nechkrappe for themselves. Survival of the strongest."* She lifts her beak boldly, as if she's proud that she survived, that her species is ruthless and unloving, yet here she is.

"Well, I can't just call you nothing, if you're going to help me and all."

"Call me whatever you like, Cyan." She pulls out a black feather and holds it in her beak, jumping forward for me to take it. *"But my help is yours."*

I take the black feather, and I can feel her magic. It's weaker now that it has been disconnected from her body, but if I am quick I will still be able to harness it.

I look up at the sky as the sun begins its descent and the stars blink into existence, the brightest of all being Hesper, the evening star. I look down at the bird and hold my arm out for her. She jumps and flaps her wings to land, her claws gently digging into my flesh but not enough to break the skin. "How about Hesper?" I ask.

She gently takes a side step further up my arm, those milky eyes wide with an innocence that surely a Nechkrappe cannot possess. *But how she looks at me...*

Gently, she runs her head under my jaw. I try not to flinch as she says, *"Sounds like home, Cyan."*

Mallrie is waiting for me on the edge of the forest. Night has well and truly fallen and Vaasis' magic seeps out from her tall branches, protecting our coven from the monsters that lurk in the dark. Something in my chest tightens when I see Mallrie's stone face. The fire elementals behind him light the last of the lanterns that hang between houses, silhouetting his figure and adding an ominous presence to his arms, folded across his broad chest. His body tenses when he sees the large black bird on my shoulder. Hesper eyes him carefully, whispering into my mind, *"Remember, Cyan, no one must know I can speak to you. Even your brother. Even if his heart is pure."* A shudder works through my body as her voice drops an octave, and her beak brushes against my ear.

"Cyan..." Mallrie whispers, his fingers twitching as if he doesn't know whether to reach out to me, the sword strapped to his back, or the dagger at his thigh.

"It's okay, Mallrie. This is Hesper." I look up at her and run my finger along her raven-black feathers. "She's a friend."

Mallrie's brows shoot up his head. "That's a Nechkrappe, Cyan," he says, stunned.

"I know. But she won't hurt us. I promise."

Mallrie blinks his eyes a few times. "I trust you, Cyan," he says. He sounds tired as he scrubs a hand over his face, and the guilt of what he has offered to help with worms its way through my body.

I should have thought this through. I shouldn't have let him get involved. Guilt consumes me, twisting my gut and leaving me feeling unsettled.

"Your brother loves you, Cyan. He would have wanted you to go to him for his help. He will support you through whatever may come. Even befriending a Nechkrappe." Hesper chuckles the last thought into my mind, yet the bird doesn't make a sound this time.

"Stay out of my thoughts!" I snap back, feeling entirely unnerved that they're now being invaded. Hesper's light laughter just filters into my mind.

"Okay. Abeline, Adriana and Alinta are with Cora and Lia." My body tenses, wondering what he told Cora to get her to agree to assist in something so unpleasant. "Mother will be... distracted for..." Mallrie's eyes glow a soft lilac as he uses magic to search for his answer. "About an hour, if we're lucky."

I nod as I hold back the knot of emotion forming in my throat. I've never doubted Mallrie's love, but we're brothers. We don't talk about our feelings; we fight and torment each other. Yet, there's an unspoken understanding and loyalty between us that goes beyond words.

CHAPTER SEVENTEEN

CYAN

The ale we drank at Erik's Tavern sits heavily in my stomach as we wait for the Enkantians to return to their homes for the evening. Erik picks up our tankards, nodding towards Vaasis and our home beyond. "I don't care who you are, I'm shutting shop now." Mallrie's laughter mirrors Erik's. I don't know how he can be so relaxed right now.

"That's fair, mate. We'll get out of your hair." Mallrie pushes to his feet, stumbling and falling back down. He's not drunk, and I narrow my eyes at him and his charade. "Give us five? We'll stack the chairs for you."

Erick runs a hand through his hair. "Alright, alright. I'm wrecked, so don't fuck anything up." He pins Mallrie with a stern stare as he walks off, leaving his beloved tavern in our care.

As soon as he is out of earshot, I turn to my brother. "*What* is going on?"

Hesper and Mallrie say 'patience' simultaneously, and it takes all of Atherton's training not to show our weaknesses to suppress my groan. "We needed to wait for everyone to be tucked away in their homes," Mallrie whispers, eyes falling to me. There's no hint of the drunken foolery that was there a moment ago when he was talking to Erik, but something darker. His words from the Melsheim Forest ring through my mind. *"Murder will fracture your soul."* I open my mouth to ask him what he meant by that, but then he says, "We don't need any witnesses."

Mallrie curses as we slowly approach our home. The warm glow of the fire brightens the windows, and a figure moves past the window. My head snaps to where Mallrie is crouched behind Vaasis, his fingers digging into the tree's bark. "I thought he'd be asleep by now."

I drag my focus away from my frowning brother to the figure in the house. "I could..." I start, but the thought falls from my tongue like morning dew on a leaf.

"Your brother has thought this through for you, Cyan," Hesper's voice whispers into my mind. I'm starting to not be as disturbed by it, which only disturbs me all the more. It's awfully confusing. *"But the drug he slipped into your father's liquor was clearly unsuccessful."*

My attention snaps back from the figure in the window, drinking deeply from the goblet in his hand. "What did you do?" I whisper-yell at Mallrie.

His cerulean eyes slide to meet mine. "I had been reading up on a spell... I thought I... Cyan, I fucked up." I can hear the anguish in his voice as he runs his fingers through his dark hair, fisting the strands at the nape of his neck.

"It's okay, Mal," I say, clapping my hand on his shoulder. "You've done more than enough." Squeezing his shoulder, I look at my hateful father, who looks like he's taken a seat by the fire like he doesn't have a care in the world. "I can take it from here."

Mallrie shakes his head, "He'll kill you, Cyan... I..." His voice wavers. "I cannot lose you."

"Ask him what he saw," Hesper whispers.

My head snaps up to where the creature is sitting in the branches of Vaasis, and by the Fates, the Nechkrappe hisses at me. I look away, too afraid to meet her milky white gaze or to ask her what she knows. Instead, I whisper. "Mal... what did you see?" he shakes his head. "You looked into the *Timeline*, didn't you?"

"He. *Will.* Kill. You," Mallrie murmurs, his voice shaking. "I won't let that happen." He turns his attention to me. "We'll do it together."

My mouth falls open. "You'd kill your own father... with me?"

"For you. You don't deserve to live in fear."

I worry my bottom lip, and Hesper swoops down from her perch, hopping closer to us. Mallrie's body tenses as her milky eyes close, and she rubs her head against his knee. "You'd take a father away from the girls?" *I didn't think this through. I was angry and selfish. If I kill him, our sisters will grow up without a father. They still need him.*

Mallrie shakes his head. "He's no father to them, Cyan. When have you ever seen him play with them? Listen to them ramble? That's what we do. We're all the family they need."

Hesper's sharp beak pecks at my kneecap, causing me to curse her name. *"Sorry,"* she whispers into my mind. *"He has had to grow up too fast. Too many responsibilities have been placed on his young shoulders. Let him help you with this. You'd be surprised how much he needs this. Just as much as you do."*

CHAPTER EIGHTEEN
MALLRIE

"I got to ask," I breathe as we slowly stumble towards our home, dread sitting heavily in my chest. "What did you promise the Nechkrappe?"

Cyan looks at me, his dark brows pressed over his eyes. "Nothing. I swear it."

There's no lie on his face, and I believe him, yet I fear that he's trading one ill fate for another. The cursed creatures are drawn to chaos and death, and the tight coil in my stomach worries for my brother's fate. "You'd tell me if something was wrong?" Now isn't the time to be having this discussion, but the Nechkrappe has been hovering close to Cyan since he appeared through the thick bushes at the edge of the Melsheim Forest.

"Of course." He walks ahead, my dagger sheathed along the waistband of his trousers. I glance over my shoulder at the milky white eyes, perched high in Vaasis's branches, seemingly glowing in the darkness.

We walk into the living space of our home. Between the heat from the fire and the nerves racing through my body, a sheen of sweat forms at the base of my neck. We walk, arms thrown across the other's shoulders, laughing boisterously and pretending to be a little merry.

"What is the meaning of this?" Atherton snaps. His words slur slightly from how much he has had to drink and the potion I slipped into his favourite liquor. "Where the fuck is everyone? Where are the girls?" he demands, crossing one long leg over the other.

I step forward, flaying my arms wide. "It's just the men tonight, Father!" The drunken mask I slipped on before entering threatens to crack at giving him the honour of being called a father. Thankfully for me, years of Atherton's torment have meant that I can lock away my emotions when I need to. "How about a drink at the tavern, aye?"

Atherton eyes me, then Cyan. "I only see two men here, and I'd never say no to a drink with my *son*."

Cyan scoffs from behind me. My eyes slide to where he leans against the wall, his arms folded across his chest.

Thankfully, Atherton ignores it. "Where's my wife?" he asks as he not so subtly readjusts himself. And now I have to reign in the snarl trying to rip from my throat like a wild ashga and the disgust bubbling in my stomach.

"There's been a *disturbance* with the lorkreigs that she needed to take care of." My tone is cold and harsh. Gone is the façade of a good time at the tavern. "Cora and Lia offered to watch the girls since I was too busy having a merry time with my *brother*."

Atherton's fist swings, but my magic is faster, snapping out my hand and catching his wrist before he can backhand me across the face. As I tighten my grip, his intense glare shifts to meet my unwavering gaze. "You need to learn some respect, Mallrie. You have responsibilities—"

I snap his hand backward, breaking the bone in two without a blink, without a lick of remorse. "Yes. I do," I growl over his roar. Wrapping my hand around his mouth, muffling his shouts, I spin around so his back is pressed against my chest.

Cyan steps forward, unsheathing the dagger, but before he can strike, Atherton's magic has pushed barbed vines through the floorboards and ripped Cyan and me away from him. Atherton whirls on me, his magic wrapping around my throat, squeezing the air from me and binding my outstretched arms.

"What. Are. You. Doing. Mallrie?" He articulates every word with lethal calmness, ambling over to me. His head cocks to the side, looking over his shoulder to where Cyan is bound on the opposite wall. "Are you... are you trying to *kill* me?" The laughter in his voice sends an ominous shiver down my spine. I gasp, trying to bring precious air into my burning lungs. "You *are* trying to kill me." His laughter is like a crack of thunder.

The edges of my vision darken as I pray to the Fates to watch over Cyan and keep him safe. The last thing to run through my mind as the darkness takes hold is that I have failed him.

CHAPTER NINETEEN

CYAN

The tang of magic sits on my tongue like a burst of citrus, humming in the air around me and pulsing through my veins in a wild beat. I've tried speaking to the elders, searching through tome after tome of earth elemental magic, and I've yet to come to some sort of reason why my magic feels like this sometimes. It's wild and primal. Sometimes I cannot control it, and that scares me.

The feral magic screams through me, reaching out like roots searching for water, calling out to Atherton's magic. His own shudders as if it's made of thin ice. My boot is pressing against the surface, but I can't break it—not yet. The metallic taste of blood presses against my lips as I grit my teeth together, continuing to push against his magic. I can feel Atherton's magic shudder against my skin, its essence cracking with every push. The vines fall limply to the floor, and I fall with them, landing on the balls of my feet.

There is a tapping at the window, and I turn to see Hesper bouncing up and down, cawing like a maniac. I fling out a hand, my magic reaching out to Mallrie to break the bindings around his neck and body. My other hand pushes open the window, and Hesper pops her head in.

"My feather. Make the bastard swallow it!"

Mallrie's body falls into an unconscious heap on the floor as the vines wither away, browning with disease.

Atherton spins on his toe to glare at me. "You *ungrateful, revolting* piece of shit!" he shouts, spit flying with each hateful word.

I snap my hand out, and one of his vines that was holding Mallrie comes to life and wraps around his head, forcing it backwards. I run and shove the black feather down his throat, calamus-first. His cerulean eyes widen as he gags on the sharp point, but the vines shift, wrapping around his head and forcing his mouth closed.

"NO!" Hesper screams in my mind, and for a second I want to turn to look at her to demand what she's screaming about, that I am doing what she told me...

Something sharp pierces me and I stumble back a few paces. I look down, unable to comprehend what I'm seeing. A leather-wrapped handle is protruding from my lower sternum. A warmth spreads through me and my knees wobble, feeling like a thousand tiny needles are poking me as I stumble back. My breath is quick and painful. No matter how hard I try to bring air into my lungs, I can't.

Azalea would laugh, seeing me struggle. I can hear it. *"You're always so good at holding your breath when I fuck you, but now, on land? Pathetic."*

My brows pinch together. *No, Azalea would never call me pathetic.* I sputter, blood spraying from my lips.

"NO!" Mallrie's muffled shout breaks me out of my stupor.

My hand wraps around the handle of the blade, more

blood spilling over my other hand as I press it around the wound.

"Do not pull it out!" Hesper shouts in my mind, yet her voice feels so far away. *"Do not pull it out, Cyan!"*

With a distant awareness, I am painfully aware that she is right. With each passing moment, the lodged blade within me causes agony that only intensifies with each laboured breath. The metallic scent of blood fills the air, mingling with the acrid smell of fear. The sight of the dagger protruding from my body sends shivers down my spine, triggering an instinctual desperation to rid myself of this foreign object.

There is a scuffle and the sound of furniture splintering. Something hard reverberates up my spine, and I realise I have fallen to the floor. My fingers slip between the inch of the blade protruding from me and press down, trying to apply pressure to the wound. My eyes refocus on the scene unfolding before me. Hesper claws at Atherton's face and back as Mallrie fights him—our father—trying to get to me. The darkness seeping in around the corners of my vision slowly takes hold, and I drift off to that place between life and death.

Vraska.

Blinking doesn't dissolve the darkness. I'm not even sure if my eyes are still open or closed. Perhaps I didn't end up in Vraska after all. Maybe this is just death. Maybe all the stories and promises of an Afterlife were just that—stories. Something to give us hope that there's something greater waiting for us after death. Not this eternal darkness with no beginning and no end. Or maybe this happens to those who don't deserve the peace of the Afterlife. Perhaps this is the fate of those who have lied, emulated, cheated and murdered.

I press a hand to where Atherton's dagger was. I can still feel the slow dribble of warm, sticky blood. It makes my fingers slick, and I idly rub them together as I look around at the disorienting space. A slow blink, and then before me stands a hauntingly beautiful woman, blocking the path towards the sudden bright light. My fingers scrape together, the blood flaking off as I gape at her long raven black hair, hanging limply around her pale face. There's a dark stain tinted around her lips, as if she's ingested something rotten. Her silver eyes sparkle even in the non-existent light.

Fear twists at my insides. *She's no Fae, so how is she here? Perhaps she's a demon, ready to drag me to hell for attempting to murder my father.*

"I am no demon, Cyan. Son of no one, born of dishonesties and deceit." Her voice is like the darkest night and crushed velvet. It's smoky and yet smooth. "I am simply here to guide you."

"But... you're not fae?" Looking around, everything appears the same. If it weren't for this woman standing before me, I wouldn't know which direction is which. The eternal darkness stretches around me, consuming everything around it. "Are you here to take me to hell?"

Her laughter is rough, like dried bones clattering in the wind. "No."

My mistake is looking away from her, hoping to see someone else. Being in her presence is unnerving, and my mind is screaming at me to run. But where would I go? I turn again, and she's standing directly in front of me. Her body is inches from mine as she looks down her nose at me. She's tall.

Her long finger stretches out. "You're not done yet." She touches my forehead and my eyes roll back into my head. The darkness tips and I feel like I am falling into the abyss.

Mallrie has our father pinned against the wall, but Atherton has one of the dead vines wrapped around his throat. It's a struggle of power. Rolling onto my side, I find Hesper standing over me, a string of curses spilling from my lips as I force myself onto my knees.

"Mal..." my throat feels like it's been stuffed with cotton. Mallrie attempts to look over his shoulder, but that gives Atherton the upper hand, and he's out of Mallrie's grip in a heartbeat.

Mallrie falls to his knees. His face is deathly pale as he rips the vines from his neck.

Atherton stalks before me, his boot raised to kick the dagger deeper into my sternum when it freezes completely mid-air.

But it's not frozen. It's moving ever so slowly. I look at Mallrie. "Hurry," he rasps. "I can't... hold it... for long."

I move out of the way. With my back pressed against the wall, I force myself to my feet and unsheathe the dagger Mallrie cursed. Its purple glow seems to pulse, as if it can sense the death hanging in the air, and it's desperate to grasp hold of it.

Time resumes and Atherton stumbles, his foot missing

its target. He turns angrily, cursing and spitting insults at Mallrie. His distraction has my boot between his shoulder blades and his body lurching forward. I pin him to the ground with my magic, though the vines are weak and brittle, constantly snapping as they push through the floorboard or attempt to tie themselves into knots.

It doesn't matter.

The enchanted blade is at Atherton's throat, and yet my hand stalls. He laughs darkly. "You always were spineless and pathetic. Couldn't even kill a hare."

As I hold the blade against his skin, I can feel his pulse quicken and his eyes widen just a fraction. I can practically taste his fear on my tongue. My wound must be making me delirious, because I chuckle in his ear. "I thought you taught us to be fearless, Father, even in the face of death."

His breathing stutters as his mask melts away, fear bleeding through his pores and reeking of death and decay.

"I may have never killed before, but that's because I had nothing worth killing for. *You* changed that. *You* changed me. *You* have created this, and I *will* kill you." Ever so slowly, I drag the blade across his throat, savouring the feel of his skin splitting open like a seam. Savouring the sounds of his muffled screams as I press my hand tightly over his mouth. Savouring the way his warm blood oozes out of the wound at his throat and over my hand. I watch the manic fear in his eyes dart from me to Mallrie—who is standing over my shoulder—pleading for help. When he finds no mercy on his eldest son's face, his eyes return to me. The fear is fading, as is the light—the life—in his eyes.

Atherton Delacroix manages one final gurgled moan before he dies.

CHAPTER TWENTY

CYAN

urder can fracture one's soul.

M I laugh, a rough, hollow sound as I fall back away from Atherton's lifeless body. Perhaps murder also fractures one's mind. I feel delirious, almost hysterical as I struggle to draw breath between bursts of laughter. "Alright," I hear Mallrie say, his hand wrapping around mine, gently removing the cursed dagger that now contains Atherton's soul. My heart is beating too loudly in my head, and the dagger in my sternum is excruciating as my brother helps me sit against the wall. "You need to focus now, Cyan. We're not out of the woods yet."

Another wave of hysteria ruptures from me, causing the dagger to shudder painfully. "But... we are... out of the woods," I chuckle breathlessly, my vision starting to blur around the corners. The weight of my head is too much as it lolls against the wall.

"Stay with me," Mallrie whispers urgently as he stuffs a piece of fabric into my mouth. I wince at the salty taste of blood and sweat. My eyes fall to where his hand has hesitated, his fingers flexing around the hilt of the dagger. As much as I'm able to, I grunt, nodding my head and closing my eyes. The sweet darkness calls me back, and I wonder if the *non*-demon will be there once again. There was something eerily beautiful about her.

Body arching off the wall, my head cracks against the wooden panels as I groan around the fabric, flashes of bright light lighting up the back of my eyelids as Mallrie slowly drags out the dagger, muttering words of encouragement. "I'm not finished with you yet, little brother. You've got this. Almost there." A scream rips from my body as the last bit of the blade is pulled. Faintly, I hear it clang against the floor, and then Mallrie is ripping my shirt open and pressing his warm palms to the wound. "Keep your *damn* eyes on me, Cyan," he growls. "We just killed him together. You're not leaving me now." I can feel his magic pour into me as he mutters an incantation under his breath, but my eyes feel too heavy to keep open. His palm slaps me across the face, forcing my eyes to pop open. "You don't die on me now, you prick!" he curses. "You've got to live a long and peaceful life now." His boots click along the wooden floors away from me, and I rest my head against the pillow he's placed behind me. A sharp, stinging pain flares where the wound is, and I groan in discomfort. "That's it, Cyan," Mallrie murmurs encouragingly. "Curse at me. Tell me how much this fucking hurts. He's not here to punish you anymore. You're free, Cyan."

He helps me sit up and I groan again, gently rubbing at the bandage Mallrie has wrapped around the stitches. I raise an eyebrow at him. Surely the dressing is overkill.

"You tend to scratch at your stitches," Mallrie says matter-of-factly. "This way, you won't accidentally rip one out like you have in the past."

My lips twitch, and then a burst of laughter rips from

my throat, tugging at my stitches and making me press a hand to my sternum to stop the ache. *But fuck! It feels so good, like a weight has been lifted from my chest.* "Thank you, Mallrie," I say between bursts of laughter.

His own lips tug at the corner, and there is a lightness in his eyes, but he doesn't join in on my laughter. "Don't thank me yet, brother. We need to dispose of the body."

Mallrie refuses to let me help him carry Atherton's corpse into the forest. I'm grateful, because I can hardly lift my own fucking arms, and the slight incline has my breath sawing through me. "We can stop if you need a breather," he says, repositioning Atherton's body. Blood has stained the back of his tunic and one sleeve is missing from where he ripped it off to stuff it in my mouth. We're almost out of the protection that Vaasis offers.

"I'm fine," I lie, my hand pressed lightly against the wound, as if at any moment the dagger could reappear. I'm no stranger to wounds. Fates, Atherton threw a dagger at me only weeks ago. My fingers move from my sternum up to my shoulder, where the serpent and rose tattoo cover the scar. I paid a healer an obscene amount to give me a herb Avark enchants to help speed up healing so I could cover the scar as quickly as possible. "Let's just get this over with."

Mallrie nods and continues walking. I follow him deeper into the forest, further away from Vaasis' protection. As soon as we cross that invisible line, all the hairs on my body rise with the danger surrounding us. The guttural clicking sound of the Kailadons echoes all around us. We don't go too far from Vaasis' protection. Just deep enough for Atherton's death to not seem suspicious.

Mallrie looks towards the sky, the stars only just visible through the thick canopy. "Do you think you'll be able to climb it?" he asks before looking behind him, as if he can see how far the protective enchantment is from here.

I follow his line of sight, saying, "I'll make that."

"Go now. I don't want to leave anything to chance. Not after the shitshow of tonight."

Reluctantly, I nod and start walking back. A fleshy thud sounds behind me as Mallrie dumps Atherton's body on the cold ground before scaling a nearby tree. "Two more paces," he calls from a high branch. If he knows Hesper is sitting in a nearby tree, he doesn't show it.

Mallrie settles in the tree, sparks of magic appearing around his fingertips as he touches his forefingers together, then his thumb, flipping his hands as he continues to do a series of hand gestures. Atherton's foot twitches and I hold my breath, my body aching with the tension forming in my arms. I regret hiding Mallrie's dagger in the floorboards under my bed. A leg spasms and then Atherton is sitting up, gasping as blood spurts from the wound at his throat.

"They're coming!" Mallrie calls, but I can already smell them. The pungent stench of death and decay as the Kailadons' raspy clicking grows louder and louder.

My muscles go taut, readying to fight, despite being behind the protective wards of Vaasis.

"You don't have to stay," Mallrie calls, his magic holding firm despite the look of exhaustion clinging to the edges of his eyes.

I know I don't, but I need to see this with my own eyes. Despite Atherton's soul now being trapped in the blade

Mallrie cursed, I need to know that his body will be destroyed as well. My gaze finds Mallrie's just as a Kailadon breaks through the bushes and drops to its knees before Atherton, its long bladed arms starting to carve off long slivers of flesh. "I'm not going anywhere."

CHAPTER TWENTY-ONE

MALLRIE

O ur small home is almost indistinguishable. Gone is the warm and cosy living space. Splintered furniture and bloody smears are all that remain. My body aches from the fight with Atherton and then sitting in the tree until the Kailadon finished devouring what it wanted of Atherton's body. Covered in dirt and sweat, I lean against the wall, feeling the rough texture against my back as I contemplate the daunting amount of work left to be done before Mother returns. I try to summon a kernel of magic to help slow time to give us a few more hours, but there are only sparks, nothing tangible enough to summon.

Cyan's leaning against the wall by the fire, his head tilted back, eyes closed. Now and then, his lips move and he mumbles something under his breath. I eye the Nechkrappe carefully. I fear he might have lost part of his mind tonight. I believed him when he said he made no deals with the bird, and yet here it is, following him like a lost puppy. That blade I gifted him; the magic that infused in the steel is strong time magic. I remember reading about the spell and all the warnings that came along with it. Warnings of sending the yielders mad.

The Nechkrappe hops along the floorboards, its beak rubbing against one of the pools of blood, and I scrunch up my nose in disgust. It looks like the bird is trying to coat its feathers in it, or perhaps it's simply trying to drink it.

"Cyan?" He looks up at me. His face is still too pale for my liking. "Do you want a drink?" I ask, moving to where our parents keep their liquor by the fireplace, needing something to distract me from the disturbing creature.

Cyan looks around the room. "Shouldn't we start... um..."

I clap him on the shoulder as I pass. "I think you have earned yourself a drink." I fill two glasses with Atherton's liquor.

Cyan gingerly takes one from my hand as he pushes himself to his feet.

"You know," I start, taking a sip of the amber liquid, "When Atherton took me out for my first kill, he also gave me a glass of liquor when we returned home." I examine the liquid dancing in the firelight. "Probably isn't the best tradition to continue. I apologise."

Probably wasn't the best tradition to begin with. I'd only just turned eight when he took me into the forest. After he heard I had killed the meshlynk, it seemed he was even more interested in seeing me kill with his own eyes.

Cyan waves his hand through the air, taking a sip. "It's fine," he grunts. "Actually, I think it's rather fitting. That we're sharing this moment. His liquor. Grumpy old bastard deserved what he got." Cyan pulls the dagger out and examines the glowing blade. Before we left, he hid it in our bedroom, but he retrieved it when we returned. It was as if he was unsettled with it being out of sight. "I know I should feel bad or sad. But honestly, I don't."

"And you shouldn't have to feel anything but relieved," I say, draping my arm over his shoulders. "Atherton was a terrible father, a questionable husband and a miserable person. The way I see it, we've done the coven a favour, ridding them of his presence."

"*That* I can drink to." Cyan clinks his glass against my own and we down the rest of our drinks before beginning to scrub the blood from the floor.

The armchair groans under my weight as I fall into its soft leather upholstery and drape my arm over my face. "I could fall asleep right here," I groan, feeling all of my exhaustion creeping up on me. The sun is just starting to creep along the horizon, and I send a silent prayer up to the Fates that we managed to right everything before people started to emerge from their slumber. However, it doesn't pass my mind that our mother never made it home last night, and there's a nervous sort of energy shifting through my exhausted body, like ants crawling just under my skin. I worry about what could have kept her out all night.

"Well, you can rest now, Mal," Cyan says, tapping my bicep with a glass of wine that I grasp with an undeniable eagerness. "You've done more than enough for me."

Shaking my head, I sigh. "I don't think so." I lean forward in the chair, elbows resting on my knees as I look into the glass. "I should have done more. You never should have been in a position where you felt you needed to kill to feel safe in your own home."

Cyan shrugs a shoulder. The colour has returned to his face, and he's looking a lot more at ease with the events that have unfolded this evening, despite the heavy bags that line his eyes and the weight of his own exhaustion, heavy on his shoulders. "Fate is a fickle thing. Isn't that what Avark teaches you?"

I hum my agreement. *That is what Avark says.*

Leaning forward in the chair, I lock eyes with Cyan, my elbows resting on my knees as I look down into the rich mulberry wine.

"I guess you're the one to take up that chair now," Cyan jokes, but his words slither along my skin like an oil that has me sliding onto the floor and scooting to sit beside him on the cushions by the fire.

"I'd rather not," I whisper, glaring at Atherton's chair. I take a sip of the wine, finding there's an acidity to it that gives it a fresh zing against my tongue. One that wasn't put there by Erik but by the thought of potentially becoming like the man who sired me.

"You'd be nothing like him," Cyan murmurs, taking a deep drink from his goblet. "Actually, I think you'd make a rather good father."

I snort into my glass. "I don't think I'll be fathering any children."

"Because of me?" Cyan whispers, catching my gaze. "Because you had to grow up too fast to look after me?"

I sigh and throw an arm around Cyan's shoulder, dragging him closer. "Perhaps," I say, a tired sigh slipping from my lips as I briefly imagine what my life could have been like without Cyan. But before those thoughts can take hold, I find myself smiling and shaking my head as I say, "But I wouldn't change it for the world. Do you know what your first word was?" I ask, still smiling at the memory. My magic thrums under my skin, a tired and desperate hum, and I let it seep into Cyan's mind.

The night creeps in through the windows, and a small, blonde-haired boy is writhing around on my bed, not at all ready to fall asleep. But the days have been long and I am exhausted. Crawling onto the bed, I wrap an arm around Cyan and pull his tiny body against mine. He giggles and plays with the small rattle I made him and the carving of a bear. The three inter-twined rings clank together, the sound grating on my fraying nerves. All I want to do is to fall asleep. I don't want to deal with a small witchling who is not ready to go to sleep. Wrapping my hand around his to stop the incessant sound, I ground out between my teeth, "Maybe this wasn't the best toy to have made."

Cyan whines as he struggles to pull the rattle free, and I can hear Atherton grumble in the main living space. He's had a lot to drink tonight, and I am too exhausted to prevent him from storming in here in a drunken rage.

Releasing Cyan, he settles, dropping the bear carving on my head so the rattle can have his full attention. I groan and bite back a curse as I move the carving to the small stool beside my bed. "It's time to go to sleep, Cyan." I yawn, barely able to keep my eyes open.

Cyan sits up, wriggling out of my embrace, and presses his hands against my face, squishing my lips and cheeks together in a fit of giggles. "Mal!" comes the garbled sound between his laughter.

My eyes snap open and I sit up, bringing the small child into my lap. "What did you say?" I whisper-yell, quickly glancing to the door to make sure everyone is out of potential earshot.

"Mal!" Cyan repeats a little clearer.

The tears that line Cyan's green-blue eyes become clearer through the purple haze as my magic wanes. A fresh wave of pride fills my chest that I meant so much to that small witchling that his first word was my name. "I was there for your first steps," I say, swallowing the knot forming in my throat. "And once you got your bearings, you were like my little shadow for years. Never—not once—did I wish any of it was different," I say, clearing my throat, forcing that bit of emotion back away and sipping from my glass. "You're my best friend."

CHAPTER TWENTY-TWO

MALLRIE

1851

There is a pounding ache behind my eyes, and my body is stiff from sitting for so long, but I school my features into a cool indifference, just as Atherton taught me to.

Don't show your weaknesses.

Fuck. It's been years since Atherton's soul was ripped from his body, never to enter Vraska or the Afterlife, and yet he's still in my fucking head. The heat of the cave is almost suffocating, yet Avark sits there reading a tome, as if he cannot feel the humidity pressing against his skin. It's only just the start of autumn, but the heat still clings to the cavern walls, and the enchanted fire only adds to the insufferable heat.

The hard stool scrapes against the stone floor as I pick up the now-restored book, dusting off the cover before I drop it onto Avark's desk. The sound of the wooden cover falling onto the desk reverberates through the cave, but he doesn't look up.

"I restored it," I say, clearing my throat.

"Have you now?"

If you looked up, you'd fucking see with your own eyes. "Yes, sir." I bite down on my irritation, breathing in deeply through my nose.

"Very good," Avark says, slowly turning the yellowing page.

I stand there. Waiting. *The fucking power trip Avark gets is ridiculous. I wonder when he'll stop demanding these lessons. Some days, I'm just going over what I already know. Other days, he's making me look into the* Timeline *without the Fates' knowledge, which always fills me with a profound sense of discomfort.*

Avark finally looks up. "What are you standing here for?"

My teeth grind together and I can feel the muscle in my jaw flex with the amount of restraint I'm holding in. "Just waiting to see if there's anything else you'd like me to do today."

"No, I think that's enough," Avark says, his eyes skimming over the cover of the book on his desk. "Same time tomorrow, Mallrie. Don't be late."

I nod once, but as I turn on my heel, I roll my eyes and collect my belongings. A shockwave of magic jolts through my body, and a flash of colours explodes before my eyes as I pass through the wards protecting the cave. As soon as I step out, the insufferable heat wanes. Not a lot, but enough for me to know the only sweat dripping down my back will be from my own exertion.

"And where did you come from?" I drawl as Winnie slinks out from behind a boulder. The small misnac trips over her large paws as she races towards me, and I scoop her up in my arms. "Have you been hiding out here, waiting for me?"

Winnie purrs and rubs her small head against me, the nubs of her horns digging into my skin through my tunic. Her claws dig into the fabric of my shirt as she climbs up my torso to sit on my shoulder. The closer we get to the training ring, the more anxious the misnac seems. She's not used to people, and it's only recently that she seems to have taken a liking to me. I open my satchel and she practically leaps into the leather bag as the sound of metal clashing becomes louder.

"I think there's some dried beef in there—" Winnie pops her head up, a piece of dried meat sticking out of her mouth. Her jaws work almost comically as she tries to chew on the tough meat. "Oh, good, you found it," I chuckle, patting her head.

Leander is overseeing one of the younger witches, tending to the weapons. I watch for a moment how he corrects the boy's grip on the whetstones so he can sharpen the blade of an axe. Smiling to myself, I carefully drop my bag on the ground next to the tally marks Cyan and I carved into the rock wall. Winnie's blood-red eyes peer out at me through the flap of my satchel, and I place a finger to my lips and watch as she shrinks back, wisps of darkness concealing her. I smile to myself as I pull my shirt over my head, knowing that she's still watching but will most likely end up asleep, covered in ink and fragments of dried meat.

Leander wanders over to me as I start my warm-ups. "Nice to see you here," he says with his hands on his hips, the grey forming in his hair illuminated in the sun.

"It was either come here or fall asleep in that unbearable heat."

"Well, maybe you could lead the witchlings through basic hand-to-hand combat?" Leander says as he watches me run through my stretches.

"Yeah, or you could do it," I say, looking up at him. "Like I asked you to."

Leander lifts a shoulder. "But you should be the one. After all, you're Atherton's son."

"He's got another son," I say, looking up at Leander to gauge his reaction. His dark brows twitch, but he does well to keep his expression concealed. "Besides," I say, resuming my stretches, "I asked you. If you don't want the position, I'll give it to Lia. Which, actually, probably isn't a bad idea," I muse aloud. "Might inspire some more females to come to training."

"She's welcome to train the witchlings," Leander mutters.

"I'm sure she'd whip their asses into line in no time..."

Leander's and my heads both turn at the same time to the sound of too-loud conversations. Enkantians know to keep their voices down when walking through the forest. Even though we've got the protection of Vaasis stretching out into the Melsheim Forest, we don't tempt the creatures to attempt to break through those wards.

My boots scrape along the dirt as I scramble towards my satchel as Leander instructs half the witches training to return to the coven and the other half to ready themselves. Slinging my tunic over my head, I whisper into the darkness of my satchel, "Winnie, go home. Don't be seen," before racing off and grabbing two short swords from the rack on my way.

Leander hides behind the tree opposite me, his hands signalling a rough estimate of how many people are wandering through the Melsheim Forest. I move through the shrubs to cut them off before they reach the barrier of Vaasis' magic, Leander on my heels. The rest of the witches stay hidden in the shadows of the large trees.

Some women shriek as Leander and I step out from our hiding places, weapons drawn but down by our sides.

"Hello," I say, sheathing one sword at my side to lift a hand. A tactic to show them that we mean no harm but won't hesitate to fight back if provoked.

The group parts and a tall man with blonde hair and a strange rounded hat steps out. I note the few weapons on his person. He says something, but I don't quite understand what. I look at Leander, who's also frowning at this stranger.

"Greetings," the man says again in a strange accent and broken Enkantian.

"Are you okay?" Leander asks, folding his arms across his chest despite still holding onto two short axes. "Your people look in a bit of a state."

The man looks between us, clearly not understanding what we're saying. I point to the two men beside him, covered in blood. "What happened?"

The man nervously looks around. A younger man steps up next to him. He could be his son. The older man looks at him before turning back to us, saying, "Flesh-Hunters."

CHAPTER TWENTY-THREE

MALLRIE

Leander and I keep our voices down. Even though the chances of these strangers being able to comprehend what we're saying is low, it's not out of the realm of possibility. "Do you believe that they're truly from the other side of the forest?" I ask.

"I don't know," Leander replies, his grip tightening on his axe. "Nevertheless, we should take caution."

I glance over my shoulder at the man who introduced himself roughly as Charleston Albatross. I think that's what he said his name was, which is a strange name for a man. "But if they're in need of assistance, we'll help."

Leander sends Kaari ahead to find the High Witchess and my sisters. Abeline is the first to find us as we return to the coven. "Hey, Mal, what's going—oh..." her lilting voice cuts off when she sees the group of people following Leander and me.

"Where's Alinta and Riri?" I ask, looking around.

"Riri is with Cora. Yes, she's baking some apple turnovers. Yes, I'm sure you can have some," she says, seemingly oblivious to the potential threat these strangers possess. "Alinta is training."

"Find your sisters. And get some food, water and blankets for Charleston's people." I motion to the masses behind us.

Abeline's blue-grey eyes shift behind me, and despite the seriousness of my tone, a small smile tugging at the corner of her lips. "Yeah, I can do that," she says with a mischievous lit to her voice.

"Abeline." Her name is rough in my throat as I grip her arm and step aside as Leander continues to lead the people through the houses to the centre of the coven, to Vaasis. Not that I wanted to congregate them all around the tree, but Leander said it'd be wise to keep them close when the High Witchess and I talk to Albatross Charleston alone. "We don't know who these people are or why they're here. Help them, but keep your distance. Do you understand?"

Abeline glances over her shoulder as women in bloodied clothes hold baskets close to their chests, their wide eyes taking in every little detail. I can see the compassion in my sister's eyes. She'll want to be with these women, helping them in any way she can, even if she cannot understand them. I can see the questions forming in her mind as her mouth opens and closes, trying to form the words. But when she returns my stare, her face is resolved into hard determination. "Don't worry, Mal. We'll be careful."

I press a kiss to her head before we part ways.

Charleston walks slowly around the living space of our home, inspecting every small detail with a scrunched-up nose. Mother stands by the fireplace in a simple, dark blue dress. The rings on her fingers sparkle in the light coming through the window as her hands are clasped in front of her. I clear my throat from my place by the door. The room isn't overly large, and even though Mother and I are standing across the room from one another, it doesn't feel awkward. "Albatross?" I say, causing both Mother and the man, who removed his odd hat upon entry, to look at me.

"Al-be*rr*t," he replies. My brows pinch together as he points to himself and says again, "Albert."

"Apologies." I truly don't give a fuck what his name is at this point. I'm more focused on how he got here.

"Albert, would you like something to drink?" Mother asks, guiding the man towards the table off to the side.

"He scarcely understands," I say, watching as he sits gracefully in the replacement of Atherton's old chair. If Mother ever realised it had been removed, she never said anything.

"A drink would be lovely," replies the man, again in a broken variation of our native tongue.

The High Witchess raises a brow at me as she walks out of the room, saying, "He seems to understand enough."

My chair scrapes across the wooden floor as I take a seat on the opposite side of the table. "Where did you come from?" I ask.

After a few hours, the language barrier becomes a little more tolerable—but still frustrating—for both parties. Mother turns to me, her tea hardly touched, but an empty glass of wine sits beside her. "Mallrie, can you please go find Avark? I believe he might know a spell to help this go a little more smoothly."

One of those words seems to click for Albert because his eyes light up as he turns to me. "Spell? Magic?"

I suppress the urge to roll my eyes. We've explained—or tried to—our magic, but he doesn't seem to fully comprehend. He mentioned something about magic and faeries' tails from where he's from, but I've never met a faerie who has a tail before.

Lifting my hand, I let my magic come to the surface, tendrils of purple smoke twining around my palm. It's nothing but an outlet for my unused magic, but Charleston recoils in his seat, his eyes wide.

A satisfied smirk pulls at my lips as I push away from the table to go find Avark. "Try not to scare the others while you're out there," Mother grumbles as I pass.

I place a kiss on her head, whispering into her ear, "Be careful."

Unease fills my chest as I walk through the crowds to find Avark. Riri is handing out small cups of water to people, and I find Alinta and Cora handing out loaves of bread. It's not until I find Abeline that the unease in my chest increases. She's with the young man who I think could be Albert's son. They're talking while she cleans a wound on his shoulder. I take a step towards them but stop. As much as I want to storm over there and tell Abeline off for disobeying me, she's really not doing anything wrong. And me losing my temper right now isn't going to do anyone any good. So, I inhale deeply through my nose, just like I've done in the past to keep my emotions in check around Atherton and keep going.

By the time I find Avark, I swear I've run into every Enkantian in the coven. Everyone is out helping Charleston's people, offering them spare clean clothes, water and food. It warms my heart to see the generosity of my people, even if it fills me with a gnawing sense of unease. Leander and his friends keep a close eye over everything, but I know it was Abeline's act of kindness that spurred on everyone else's. Again, I'm left with that feeling of wanting to reprimand and thank her equally.

The only person I don't see is Cyan. Avark turns to me when he realises I've stopped walking. "Everything okay?" he asks, leaning on his cane.

"Yes, go ahead. There's something else I need to do quickly before I return." I don't wait for Avark to reply before I'm cutting through the pathways between the houses and back to the forest. *I swear to the Fates, if he's with that mer...*

The forest's canopy blankets the flora in a gloomy glow. I don't want to be away from the coven, but I also need to make sure Cyan is safe. Something about Charleston's arrival isn't sitting well with me.

It's not long before I hear a familiar rustling, and then something fleshy falls into the grass before me. A black shadow swoops down from the tree to land at my feet. Milky white eyes look up at me as the Nechkrappe looks up at me, an eyeball in its mouth.

"Hello, Hesper."

The large black bird flings its head back and swallows the eyeball. I look around. Usually, the cursed creature isn't too far from Cyan, and despite him telling me it cannot understand him, there's something about the way I've caught him speaking to it that makes me believe otherwise.

"Look, I have little time." The Nechkrappe makes a strange sound in the back of its throat that sounds eerily similar to a scoff, which again makes me wonder if it can understand me. "I still don't trust you. And I still don't believe that you can't understand me. In the chance that you do, I need you to go find Cyan and somehow convey to him that he needs to haul ass home. Something's come up and I need him."

CHAPTER TWENTY-FOUR
CYAN

There's a change in the air. It's in the subtle fragrance of the spring flowers gently unfolding in the breeze. It's in the way the mornings become less frosty and witchlings wake earlier to play under Vaasis. Spring is all about new beginnings, but there's something fraught in the air this morning. The trees are restless. I can feel their roots shifting beneath the surface anxiously. Mallrie's occupied this morning with lessons with Avark, and the girls are busy with Cora and Lia. I didn't bother asking what they were up to this morning as Cersei was nearby, quietly talking with Cora. As much as I like and owe a great lot to the fire elemental, I won't go out of my way to be put in Cersei's line of fire.

I wander through the Melsheim Forest, my fingers brushing over the flora as I pass, sensing something is off. I'd like to talk to Esmerelda to see if she can sense it, but I won't. Even if Atherton is gone, it doesn't mean everything is all sunshine and rainbows, as I think Mallrie thought my life would become. Cersei still makes it known that my presence is a burden on her, and the rest of the coven still keeps a respectable distance.

Not that it bothers me much anymore.

At least, I try not to let it bother me much.

The clearing comes into view as the trees thin and the water sparkles, and as if she knew I was coming, Azalea sits on the bank, running her webbed fingers through her long blonde hair and sunning her tail. I knock on the hardcover book in my hand, not that I need to announce my presence. The mer sitting on the bank would have heard me approaching. If not, she would have scented me.

Azalea smiles sweetly at me. "Mind if I sit?" I ask, waving my book in the air, unable to stop the smile that spreads across my face when her eyes light up.

"Only if you read to me," she says, flicking her long golden and green tail in the air, sending droplets flying into the sky like a hundred shimmering gemstones, a pair of legs appearing in its place.

"I don't know, Az. This one doesn't have a happy ending."

She plucks the book out of my hand and turns it around in her hands, flicking through the pages, hoping to find some illustrations. "It also doesn't have any pretty pictures this time," she says with a little pout.

"Easier for you to focus on the words then," I say, pulling my tunic over my head and offering it to her. She looks as if I just handed her a dead rabbit. "You're distracting, love."

Azalea's cheeks burn bright as she reluctantly takes it from my outstretched hand. "So smooth with the compliments."

I bring her close and our bodies press against each other as if we were made for each other. "Only for you," I whisper, and I mean it. There's never been another. Not after my revelation that any Enkantian would only want me as some sort of act of defiance. Az sees me for who I am and loves every broken, fucked up piece of me. My lips brush across hers, tasting like river water. Her lips part, allowing me in. Her sharp teeth gently bite my lip and I groan, feeling my cock swell in my pants.

"I thought you were going to read me a not-happily-ever-after story," Az whispers against my lips.

"The book is not going anywhere," I say, tossing it aside, one hand sliding around her hip, the other diving into her thick hair.

Azalea pulls back, tugging against my heartstrings. I release her hair, afraid I've done something she doesn't want. "But I am." Her eyes turn sad as they take in every inch of my face. "We've been asked to go to the Fae Realm. I leave at sundown."

A knot forms in my throat. "How long will you be gone?"

"Not long... I hope. Three days? A week?"

The sight of the book amidst the grass and colourful wildflowers holds my gaze. "I should have brought you a happier book," I mutter.

A soft, webbed hand touches my cheek, guiding me back. "Not all stories end with a happily ever after, Cyan. It's what happens before the end that's important."

I kiss her again, this time soft and tender. "Then we better find out what happens."

The moments spent with Azalea by the lake are beyond words. It's as if the Fates slow time in this clearing, carving out space and time just for us, closing a veil around us to block out the world. It's not until Hesper's raspy caw sounds high above us that Azalea sits up, muttering, "Thank Ursleaam," as she drops the book on her chest.

"Don't think you're getting out of finishing the story," I say, shifting her weight against me as I sit up a little straighter against the tree I was leaning on. The moss I summoned covers the rough bark, making it more comfortable.

"But I already know how it ends, and it *was* sad. Don't make me relive that."

I smile at her little pout. "You were the one who asked me to teach you to read Enkantian," I remind her as I look for where Hesper has landed among the trees.

"Sorry to interrupt. Nice to see you both clothed for once," Hesper speaks into my mind. If she talks to Az, she doesn't make a show of responding; the mer just crosses her legs, hunches her back over the book and attempts to silently form the words written on the pages.

"It's okay," I reply to the large Nechkrappe that I barely spot in one of the trees. *"Is everything okay?"*

"Mallrie is looking for you. Something has... come up. I think it best if you return home."

CHAPTER TWENTY-FIVE
CYAN

Before the coven becomes visible, I can already feel a change in the air. The paths, once hidden under a lush carpet of flora, have been completely destroyed by careless footsteps. The Enkantians know where the paths are. They know these lands. Whoever has trampled the plants is unfamiliar with the area. The roots still carry a sense of unease along with a tinge of melancholy.

The light pierces through the trees and my body stiffens at the first signs of the coven. My hand instinctively seeks the sheathed cursed blade at my side that Mallrie gifted me, its weight and familiar grip providing a strange comfort after ten long years. The coven is abuzz with movement. Enkantians hand out blankets and warm meals to... another coven, I assume.

I keep my head down as I make my way towards the centre of the coven, towards Vaasis and home. To Mallrie.

Adriana finds me first, shortly followed by Alinta. "They're not witches," Alinta whispers in a conspiratorial voice.

"What do you mean?" I ask, looking around, still trying to find Mallrie and our other sister, Abeline.

"They're..." Alinta shrugs, a blush creeping across her face. "They don't have magic. They're from the *other side* of the forest."

"Impossible." *How would they make it through without magic? The creatures within the forest are as vicious as the demons in hell.*

"Is Abeline still talking to *him?*" Adriana asks, a touch quieter.

My head whips around to her, my eyes narrowing. *"Who?"* The word is rough as it slides between my teeth.

The two sisters giggle, looking at each other but not answering my question. Sighing, I press my fingers to the bridge of my nose, tilting my head back. "Where the fuck is Mallrie?" I ask.

"He's with the High Witchess and the... *leader* of these people," the last voice I expected to hear says behind me. My shoulders stiffen as I turn to find Leander standing behind me, Enkantian leathers and two long swords strapped down his back, a pair of daggers attached to his thick thighs.

"Where did they come from?" I ask quietly, disbelieving what Alinta said about them coming from the other side of the forest.

"Miss Alinta is right. They claim they came from the other side. They bring paintings and stories not from here *or* within the forest."

My eyes track over Leander's large body. "You don't trust them?"

"I don't trust their story." I follow his gaze over the people huddled around Vaasis. "For if what they said is true, and they came from the other side, without magic, there surely would have been more casualties."

"How do you know they didn't suffer more casualties?"

Leander's hand tightens on the handle of his axe at his side, and I have to keep my smirk trapped behind my neutral expression as I know I've hit a nerve. "Because I do," is all Leander snaps back, his eyes narrowing as if he doesn't have to explain his reasoning to someone like me. I scoff and turn to head towards our home, where Mallrie is with Cersei and one of these... people. A strong hand lands on my shoulder. "I can't let you go in there."

I knock his grip away. Baring my teeth, I growl, "I don't *fucking care*. My brother's in there."

Leander steps forward, crowding me. "I don't *fucking care*," he hisses back. "I have orders from the High Witchess *and* Mallrie. So stand the fuck down, Cyan, before you do something you'll regret."

The book groans in my grip and my magic pulses, but something soft grazes my arm, a sweet voice calling up to me. "Come on, Cyan. Let's go to Erik's." Adriana gently pulls my arm, encouraging me to walk away from the warrior before me. "Come on," she whispers again, but all I can think about is why Mallrie wouldn't want me there. *Hesper said he needed me*. Adriana pulls again, and this time my feet shift from their frozen place in front of Leander. "There you go. I'll buy you a drink."

CHAPTER TWENTY-SIX

MALLRIE

"Are you sure we can trust them?" I ask, pacing in front of the fireplace. The sun has set and Charleston's people have taken shelter in the spaces of those who've opened their homes to them. Cyan leans against the archway that leads to the back bedrooms while Lia stands behind Cora, who sits at the table with her brother Leander and Mother. I extended an invitation to them to join us for dinner since Mother decided to let Charleston and his people stay.

"You have such little faith in others, Mallrie. I thought I'd taught you better," Mother says, levelling me with a pointed stare. "I wonder if taking a break in your mentoring was the right decision."

Her words cause my feet to stop wearing a path in the floorboards. Heat flushes my cheeks and I catch Cora giving me a sympathetic look behind the High Witchess' back. "I feel I've got just reasoning not to trust them," I reply coldly. "They just appear through the forest? Why? Charleston says he's an explorer, but I think there's more to it than just academics. How did they know some Enkantian if they're from the other side?" There's so many questions left unanswered. Though Avark was able to bridge the communication gap, Charleston still seemed to keep a tight lip on some of his responses.

"If he encountered another coven, they may have mentioned something about us," Cora suggests with a shrug of her shoulder. I give her a weak smile for trying to help ease my worries.

"It doesn't matter," Mother says, pushing from her chair. "I decided we'd give them shelter. I feel like we could learn a great deal from them. There's no harm in letting them stay."

"Could be some harm," a quiet grumble comes from behind me, where I know Cyan is standing in the shadows. Unfortunately for him, he spoke loud enough for everyone to hear.

Leander scoffs, and Mother whips her head around to where Cyan is leaning against the wall, the shadows covering half his face. "Well, nobody asked for your opinion, so I suggest you either return to your room or keep your mouth shut."

"He's got a point though, Mother," I say, crossing my arms and stepping between the two of them. "They seem to age differently to us. They have no magic. And we've got no knowledge of where they've travelled from. Yes, Charleston hasn't given us a reason *not* to trust him, but I think a little caution wouldn't hurt."

CHAPTER TWENTY-SEVEN
MALLRIE

1852

Outside, a thick blanket of snow covers the land, clinging to the bare branches of Vaasis and forming delicate icicles that hang from rooftops. Even though I'm still curled up in bed, the darkness gripping the corners of the room, I know what awaits me outside. It's my favourite time of year—especially since tonight's the night we celebrate Wyntesstval, the longest night of the year. The one night a year that the Fates aren't weaving all the different threads of the future. So, we too stop and celebrate and give thanks to the them for the magic they've gifted us with and all they continue to gift us.

Winnie is curled up against my side, purring softly. I don't want to get out of bed—especially since the sun hasn't risen, though it should already have. She's so soft and content. Adriana has enchanted our home this winter to keep it warm, and I'm grateful that the job has now been taken off me. I never enjoyed manipulating the time of homes to keep them warm.

"Are you awake?" Cyan calls from the bed that's now too small for him on the opposite side of the room.

"Yeah. I should be up, but..." I let the words hang in the air between us. It doesn't feel the same to celebrate since Charleston's people settled in. It's been a few months since their surprise arrival, yet I still feel uneasy about it. Allowing Charleston and his people to join in on our festivities feels... odd. There is no trace of magic in them. They don't put their devotion in the Fates or believe that they're who control our destiny. Their belief is in the existence of two divine entities—Vid, the God of Death, and Achel, the God of Life.

"Yeah, I know." Cyan yawns and I catch a glimpse of a tattooed arm messing up his hair that's fallen out of the knot on top of his head. "But..." the word is stretched out as he sits up, stretching his arms above his head. "Someone's got important High Witch duties to attend to."

I roll my eyes. "Not really. I'm only assisting, remember?" Mother added an extra emphasis on that last night. Though I do not possess the magic of all five elementals, Cora said she'd gift me a kernel of her magic for the lighting of the ceremonial bonfire.

"Still, she's finally giving you some responsibilities. That must feel good, yeah?"

My chest constricts at his words, and I slip out from under the blanket, leaving Winnie to continue to sleep. This is what I should want, what I've prepared for and anticipated for a long time, and yet... there's a part of me that isn't as happy as I expected to be. Perhaps it's because I've already broken the vows I've yet to swear. Perhaps, deep down, I know I am not worthy.

The lighting of the bonfire was a success, even if it took me two attempts at using Cora's magic to ignite it. Witchlings run around with enchanted sticks that spark purple and blue flames for a short period, while others enjoy warm mead and my favourite honey-roasted nuts. Cora finds me shortly after the ceremony with a glass of mead and an apple pastry. "You did wonderfully," she says, despite mother's earlier words being the exact opposite. But I hold my tongue and the denial that's set there.

"Thanks, Cora," I say, the spiced drink warming my stomach. My brows pinch together slightly. "Did you put something in this?" I ask, raising a brow.

Cora shakes her head. "No. It's the same as always—oh, wait. No, Albert came to me the other day when we were preparing the mead. Said he wanted to feel included, so he helped, adding a few spices from his home on the other side."

I scrunch up my nose as I look down into the cup at the rich mulberry-coloured mead.

"Don't you like it?" Cora asks, drinking from her own cup.

"It's fine," I admit. "Just... different."

CHAPTER TWENTY-EIGHT

MALLRIE

1855

The leaves on Vaasis are a vibrant green, white buds slowly unfurling in the warm sunshine. "I'd like to have a word with you, High Witchess," the mortal man, Albert Charleston, sneers at my mother. We stop in our tracks and I turn to glare at him. Albert's blonde hair shines in the sun from the oil he's used to slick it back out of his face. He's also forgone his usual peculiar little hat that he wears. I've caught the triplets using Alinta's air magic to flick the tiny hat from his head a few times. It is very amusing, but alas, Mother has made me reprimand them for it.

My mother turns to look at him, a serene smile tugging at the fine lines around her eyes and mouth, making her face look tired and worn. She's mentioned a few times that she's been thinking about stepping down as High Witchess, but doesn't think that now is the best time with our guests taking up residence with us.

I fold my arms across my chest. For the amiable smile my mother has, my face is more of a grimace. I do not trust this man. From the moment Charleston and his people stepped through the forest, an unwelcome force of nature, to the meeting we had in our home with him and every single day since. The temptation to look into the *Timeline* is far too tempting, but I know better than to tempt the Fates.

Charleston's aquamarine eyes find mine. "Do you mind?" he snaps, the pleasantries in his voice slipping away. "I'm trying to have a conversation here." He waves his hand as if to dismiss me.

"Whatever you have to say to the High Witchess, you can say in front of me, Charleston," I snarl, allowing my magic to rise to the surface, lilac flames flickering in my eyes. His eyes widen, his feet involuntarily shuffling backwards over the gravel. Little does he know, all I am doing is providing an outlet for my magic, but it makes for a good show of the power that the Enkantians possess. I relish in the way he cowers, how his body folds in on itself despite his best efforts to steel his spine and straighten his shoulders.

"Calm yourself, Mallrie," Mother says, placing a warm hand on my arm. She lifts her chin, somehow managing to look down her nose at me even though I'm a head taller than her. "Charleston and his people are our guests." Her smile doesn't waver as she returns her gaze to the man before us.

Because, for once, you found a scrap of kindness in your heart, I think and instantly regret it. Cersei Delacroix isn't an inherently evil person, unlike our father. She remains committed to the coven without hesitation, always prioritising their needs above her own and warmly welcoming those in need into her home, as her responsibilities as the High Witchess dictate. Except for her own son. Some days, I fear that murdering Atherton just transferred some of his evil into her. Ever since she found his body mauled in the forest, she's been... distant, cold.

"Mallrie," Mother's gentle voice pulls me from the spiral of dark thoughts. "Why don't you go find your sisters? Make sure that they are not getting into any mischief, hm?"

I look between her and the smug smile on Charleston's face. He quirks an eyebrow as if challenging me. Challenging me to refuse an order from not only my mother, but my High Witchess. "Fine," the word slips between my teeth, but I make no move to walk off just yet.

"Splendid. How about we talk inside, Charleston? I can make a pot of tea," she suggests, extending her arm towards him. He hesitates for a moment, as if afraid of touching her, but eventually takes it. I watch them walk towards Vaasis, her leaves a vibrant green at the height of summer. My stomach twists on itself and I decide that before I go check on the girls, I'll pop by Cora and Lia's. I could do with one of Cora's apple pastries and her gentle ear to listen to my concerns about this mortal man and the army of people he's brought with him.

The aroma of cinnamon and buttery pastry mingled with simmering apples fills the home as Cora places a fresh pastry before me, my mouth watering at the sight of it. "Do you want some tea, too?" she asks as she returns to the kitchen.

"Only if you want a cup," I reply, panting around a mouth of searing hot apples and flaky pastry.

Her laughter is like a burst of sunshine in the darkest winter. "Maybe a glass of water?" she calls from the kitchen. "You haven't changed, Mallrie."

"Can you blame me?" I ask, lifting a shoulder in a half-shrug, taking another bite and burning my tongue once more. "You're to blame. If you didn't make the best food in the coven, I wouldn't inhale it every chance I get."

The delicately carved design on the teapot is illuminated by a faint orange glow as two ceramic cups are placed on the table. Cora's magic makes the stars and constellations on the teapot look like they're alive. Her scarred hands take the handle and pour the tea. "Don't look at me like that, Mallrie," she says sadly.

"Like what?" I ask, forcing some lightness into my voice, a smile on my face. "With love? Impossible. I love you, Cora. You're stuck with me."

Cora smiles, but it doesn't reach her eyes. "With *pity,* Mallrie. I get that enough from Lia. I'm happy with my life. *Really.*"

"I know," I say, resting an elbow on the table and scrubbing a hand over my beard. My thumb lingers on the scar on my lip. "I just hate to see your magic going—"

"To what, Mallrie?" Cora asks, dragging the plate of steaming pastries out of my reach. "I thought you loved my cooking."

"Hey, hey, hey!" I say, pushing to my feet and reaching across the table to pluck another pastry from the pile. I'm no longer the kid whose arms were too short to reach the desserts when Cora would tease me and pull them out of my reach. "Don't be doing that." I bite into the flaky goodness. "I just mean you've got a lot of talent."

"Mallrie. Stop. I *tried*. You were there. I don't want to do that with my life. Not anymore."

"Okay, Cora. Consider it dropped."

We fall into companionable silence while we finish our tea and I eat another two pastries. "I'm nervous, Cora," I say quietly. After all these years, I am still afraid to voice my insecurities in case Atherton can somehow overhear me.

"Because of Charleston and his people?" I nod, and Cora's warm hand slides over my arm, squeezing gently. "Aren't you the one who's constantly telling the coven to put their fears of someone's differences aside?"

I huff a snort because she's right. I do tell people that, but Cyan isn't dangerous. "But we know nothing about them."

"Charleston seems to be very forthcoming with sharing stories and skills from beyond the forest." Cora pushes to her feet, moving to a small shelf between the kitchen and living space that is filled with books where she's written all her recipes and those her mother and Mimi taught her. "Have a look for yourself," she says, handing me some parchment bound with twine. I eye her carefully before reading the different recipes Charleston has written for her to try. "Sometimes, we just need to trust in the plans the Fates weave," Cora says kindly.

Her faith doesn't help ease the feeling of dread sitting in my chest.

CHAPTER TWENTY-NINE

MALLRIE

"What in the Fates' names do you think you're doing?" My voice echoes over the gust of wind whipping around me. Adriana, Alinta and Abeline are definitely up to mischief, and I wonder if I should have heeded Mother's advice and gone to find them instead of going to Cora's first.

Adriana is still standing on the thatched roof of the Beaumonts' home, Abeline having jumped mere moments before I arrived, praying to the Fates that Alinta's magic would catch her on a gust of wind and bring her down safely.

Even after I shouted at them, Adriana called out a final, *"Catch!"* as she threw herself from the roof so they could all stand before me.

The three girls—who are entering early womanhood and testing my patience more than I think Cyan ever did—stand in a row. Their big, blue eyes blink up at me, their hands entwined behind their backs, the perfect picture of chaotic innocence.

"We were just having a little fun," sings Alinta. "You're the one always saying that we need to practise our magic."

I press my fingers to the bridge of my nose. "This is not what I meant," I sigh. "You could have hurt—"

Adriana skips forward and links her arm with mine, turning me away from her sisters. "We were fine, brother. You need to stress less."

"Oh! I have a great idea! Come on!" Abeline exclaims, her voice filled with excitement. The sisters share a knowing look, and together, they steer me down one of the dirt paths that all lead towards Vaasis.

I dig my heels into the dirt. "Whoa! No way I am taking you three to the tavern!" I lift my arms, pulling Abeline and Adriana clean off their feet. They squeal and giggle in delight. Alinta jumps onto my back and flings her arms around my throat. My knees almost buckle under the unexpected weight, but I hold firm.

"Alinta, you're choking me," I grit out. Thankfully, she readjusts her grip, but she doesn't climb off me.

"Oh, come on, Mal. You know Erick doesn't mind us having one or two ales there." Adriana pleads her case.

"Yeah. Besides, Mother lets us have two glasses of wine at dinner!" chimes in Alinta.

That's because Mother has become a little too friendly with the drink. I can't help but blame myself for that. Just another mistake when I've only tried to protect my family, to make them happy. Ever since Cyan and I murdered Atherton and staged his death, Mother started to end her days at the bottoms of a few too many bottles of wine.

Thankfully, Cyan swaggers around the corner, a pleased smile plastered on his face, his hair tousled and falling out of the damp knot on the top of his head, a chirpy Hesper flying above like a vulture looking for its next victim.

The girls quickly jump off me and stand behind me. As much as Cyan and I have reassured the girls that Hesper means them no harm, they're still terrified of the Nechkrappe, having been told the stories and legends about the creatures.

"Looks like someone had a good roll in the sack," I drawl, and the girls exclaim their disgust and whack at my back and side, which only makes me laugh harder.

Cyan's cheeks blush as he tucks a strand of his hair behind his ear. "You could say that," he winks.

"Cyan, tell Mal to come with us to the tavern!" Apparently feeling quite brave in the presence of Hesper, Adriana skips from behind me to interlock her arm with our brother's. But I notice her quick glance up at the Nechkrappe, as does Cyan. Then, Hesper is flying off towards the Melsheim Forest. A shudder crawls along my skin, prickling the flesh. It's unnerving how they seem to be able to communicate, even though Cyan has never confirmed that they can.

"Sounds like fun. Why are we waiting around?" Cyan's dark brows pinch together slightly, looking for why we're all not already an ale deep and dancing on Erick's tables.

"Because they're underage," I reaffirm.

Cyan waves his hand in the air, heading towards the tavern. "Pfft, as if that ever stopped us."

Giving in, I roll my eyes and follow my four siblings. "Um, actually, you didn't drink until you were sixteen. And if you remember, you threw up all over my bed."

The girls erupt into a fit of giggles and sibling teasing. "Oh, Fates, are you serious?"

"Cyan! That's so gross!"

"Ha! Seriously, Cy? You couldn't hold a simple ale?"

My arm envelops Cyan's head and I gently ruffle his

hair with my knuckles, instantly transforming from a reluctant authoritative figure to a caring brother. He pushes me away before pulling me back into his side, whispering, "One ale only." He winks. "I made sure Erick knows not to give them any more, and to let me know when they come in and flirt with him for a good time."

I wince a little at his words. I really don't want to know what my little sisters do with their spare time, but I am grateful that Cyan looks out for them when I cannot. The coven is still hesitant about his presence, even after all this time, but I know Erick would take his word seriously.

Alinta, Adriana and Abeline don't need any liquor to have a good time. They've hardly touched their ale, and they're on top of the table, dancing and singing at the top of their lungs to the mortal songs. Apparently, they've spent enough time with the young lad playing the fiddle in the corner.

Leaning back in my chair, I eye the man. His bow sits in the crook of his fingers as they deftly pluck at the strings before he swings it back around and moves it with speed and precision, building the song into a crescendo. He sings along with the girls, looking up at Abeline as if she hung the stars herself.

"That's Jeremiah Charleston," Cyan whispers. "Albert's son," he clarifies, draining his ale and reaching for one of the girls.

"I don't like the way he's looking at her," I say around

my glass. Cora could ease some of my nerves about Charleston and his people spending time with our coven, but I don't think any soothing words can calm this storm of nerves building in my chest.

Cyan chuckles. "You and me both, brother."

Somehow, that makes me feel a little better. I am not alone in this uncomfortable feeling, knowing that other men are looking at my sisters as not just the girls they once were, but now the young women that they are becoming, and having indecent thoughts. Something feral uncurls in my throat as I bite down a growl, glaring at Charleston's son.

"I've chatted with him, you know." Cyan takes a cautionary sip of the ale before spitting it back into the glass and pushing it across the table.

I raise my eyebrow at him and say, "No, I didn't." I look from the ale to Cyan, a silent question in the air.

He chuckles. "Half-strength." He waves his hand in the air, catching the bartender's attention and signalling for two more ales.

I chuckle under my breath. "Erik must be afraid you'll curse him with your Nechkrappe," I chuckle.

Cyan rolls his eyes playfully. "Or maybe he doesn't want to get in the future High Witch's bad books."

We laugh at the possibilities, at the absurd rumours we've heard recently about Hesper and Cyan. When our laughter subsides, I jerk my chin towards Charleston's son. "What are your thoughts on Jeremiah?" I ask.

Cyan shrugs. "He is definitely an improvement to his father, but I still don't trust him as far as I can throw him."

We both thank Erick as he places the drinks on the table, even going the extra mile to turn the glass so the handle faces my right side, ready to grab. Cyan gives me a knowing look.

"Neither do I," I say, watching how Jeremiah laughs at whatever Abeline is saying. "I don't trust any of them."

CHAPTER THIRTY
CYAN

The tavern is alive with music and laughter, Enkantians and Charleston's people playing instruments and singing together in a clashing harmony that somehow works. It makes me wonder if perhaps, one day, we'll be able to blend our two cultures and find a way to live harmoniously side by side. Mallrie and I clink our tankards together after raising a toast to Erik in thanks. The cool ale slips down my chin as we race to the bottom.

"Mallrie, Alinta, Abeline and Adriana Delacroix!" Our mother's voice booms in the dimly-lit tavern, her tongue scrambling over the girls' names. I almost choke on my drink at her thundering voice. It's no surprise she didn't include me in the mix, but it doesn't bother me as much anymore. Or I try not to let it bother me. The music has stopped abruptly and people glance uneasily at her. "Home. Now." Her tone is firm, a hint of anger in it.

My brows press together as I drain the last of my ale and push to my feet, along with Mallrie. We exchange glances. I guess he also has a hunch that it will not be a pleasant conversation when we return home.

Cersei says something to the patrons of Erik's tavern, but I don't hear what. Adriana slides under my arm, whispering, "She sounds *really* mad. Can you tell her we hardly touched the drinks?"

I wrap my arm around her and gently squeeze. "I don't think this is about the drink, Riri," I whisper, angling my body as we pass our mother so that Adriana is behind me. The cool night air is a whisper against my skin. Hesper quickly finds us. A dark shadow looms over us, her wingspan wide as she glides across the moon.

"Ugh!" Adriana shrinks into me as Hesper lands on my opposite shoulder. "Why does that thing follow you around like it's lost?"

I sigh. "Her name's Hesper, Riri, and because she was lost." *Hesper won't hurt the girls, I know that. But I also don't like that I cannot tell them the truth.*

Hesper told me it doesn't bother her much anymore. *"When you hear people curse you enough, you either believe it or ignore it. I chose the latter."*

I just wish I could say the same thing.

Adriana looks up at me, eyes wide. Behind her, groups of Enkantians are chatting and laughing with Charleston's people. "Like calls to like, I suppose," I mumble, my stomach twisting as I wonder how the coven has welcomed these strangers so easily while still keeping a distance from me. I slip that mask of arrogant indifference in place to hide the fact that it bothers me.

"Cy, you were never lost," Adriana says, pressing her fist into my stomach. "Mallrie was always with you. And so are we."

I smile down at her. "Then I am pretty damn lucky, aren't I?"

Her smile is infectious and she flicks her long dark hair. "I'd say so. After all, I am pretty wonderful company."

Vaasis is still glowing from the monthly ritual. Small Fae scouts hide out in her branches. Usually, some of them would come through from their realm and celebrate the ritual. They didn't come. They've been keeping their distance since Charleston's arrival, and something tells me we should be, too.

Pacing in front of our home is the small misnac that Mallrie and I found last winter. She's grown a lot since we found her, but Mal says she's still got a lot more growing to do. Her horns are mere spikes poking out of her fur. Her paws are too big for her lithe body, and she trips over them when she spots Mallrie. Four red eyes land on him, and she races towards him, bouncing like a rabbit in winter, trying to keep its paws out of the snow. She's a little clumsy and face-plants it a few times, which has her hissing at herself. Finally, Mallrie scoops the small creature into his arms, and she purrs happily.

"Like calls to like, so it seems, Hesper's sweet voice calls into my mind, mimicking my earlier words back to me like a mockingjay.

"Mallrie was never lost," I reply. *"He was always loved."*

"Are you sure about that?" Hesper asks.

"Yes?" Uncertainty mixes with the ale in my stomach, making me feel a little nauseous.

"Being loved and feeling lost can coexist, Cyan." Her voice is sweet yet sad. I want to ask her more, but I get a feeling that now isn't the right time.

I hadn't noticed that Adriana had pulled me to the pillows with her, her body pressed against mine tightly, as if afraid of our mother's impending wrath.

Cersei looks over her children sitting before her as she

stands beside Atherton's empty chair. Her eyes fall onto mine. "What are you still doing here?" she snaps.

"Apologies, Cersei. I was under the impression that I still lived here." I speak slowly and lazily. Adriana squeezes my arm in warning, her hands heating to the point of discomfort, but I don't flinch, lest our mother thinks it's her words wounding me.

She scoffs, muttering, "Not by my choice."

Mallrie enters the room without Winnie, running his fingers through his hair, and goes to sit next to Alinta.

"Here, Mallrie," Cersei says, tapping her jewelled hand on the back of the chair.

Mallrie physically winces as he straightens and sits in the chair. His eyes widen slightly, and he slowly shakes his head. I turn my attention to find Winnie sneaking out of our bedroom, having used her magic to slip through the door. I try to repress the smile tugging at the corners of my lips.

No matter how many times Mallrie tries to keep her locked away, she slips through solid objects as if they are nothing. I catch her under her soft belly as she passes by me and deposit her into Adriana's lap, who drops her face into the creature's neck and shushes her quietly. The small misnac curls up in her lap and purrs softly as Adriana becomes a small furnace next to me. I shift away from her slightly, and she throws me an apologetic look.

Mallrie and I were out with the hunting party when Hesper spotted the misnac in one of their traps. Mallrie quickly detangled her while Hesper and I threw the rest of the group off her tracks. We then spent the next month hiding the small magical creature, in fear that the coven would have her executed in fear of another war. Winnie hasn't left Mallrie's side since unless bribed with smoked meats.

"We have a situation," Cersei's voice is hushed. "Alinta, dear, make sure no one can hear us, will you?"

Alinta nods and moves her hands before her, twisting her fingers and summoning her magic. "You're good," she whispers, but her focus is only half in this room.

"Good," Cersei clips. "Albert Charleston wishes for me to stand down as High Witchess and for all magic to be stopped immediately."

Adriana and Abeline have broken into a chorus of outrage. Alinta is half-heartedly airing her grievances. Mallrie is just sitting there, his dark brows furrowed, staring at me but not seeing me. A shimmer of purple coats his cerulean eyes. Mother raises her hand, silencing the girls. "Of course, I told him no. It's preposterous and down-right insolent for him to even bring it up—"

Mallrie suddenly pushes to his feet. "Cyan," he says, an air of urgency to his tone, and I move to my feet and follow him towards the front door.

"Where do you think *you're* going?" Cersei snaps, but Mallrie ignores her and pulls open the front door. There is the zap of magic against my skin and a whoosh of air as we step through Alinta's magic.

As soon as the door is closed, Mallrie presses a hand to my shoulder and whispers, "Where's Hesper?"

CHAPTER THIRTY-ONE

CYAN

The coven has erupted into chaos. Charleston's people and Enkantians are screaming, and there is carnage everywhere we look. Hot blood oozes over my hand and splashes against my face as I slit the mortal's throat with my sword.

"CYAN!"

I spin to find Lia surrounded by mortal men, swinging two short Dane axes, fending off their attacks. But like me —like the rest of our coven—she's weak, tired.

I sprint towards her, jumping over the dead and cutting down anyone I can in my path.

My sword sinks deep into the man and a gurgling sound fills his throat as I toss his body aside. Gritting my teeth, my sword clashes with one of Charleston's men. My eyes widen, a feral growl ripping from my throat, and the earth shudders under my feet. *"You,"* I snarl, summoning all of my strength and willing my magic to come back. But the poison is too strong.

Jeremiah smiles at me, his teeth coated in blood.

"Why?" The question is out of my mouth before I can stop it.

"Why?" He parrots, his eyes filled with malice. "Because my father says so. The king says so." His boot lands in the centre of my chest, knocking me back a few steps and winding me. "This land is to be in the name of the king. If your *High Witchess* won't bend her knee, then she shall fall!"

I force myself to my feet, charging at Jeremiah with a battle cry so primal that I don't recognise it on my tongue. Our swords clash and our feet move in a dance.

"I wonder," Jeremiah muses, sweat dotting his brow, "once I kill you and the rest of your coven, how much Abeline will submit to me. Will she still look at me with that fire of desire in her eyes? Or will I just have to fuck her into submission, hm?"

I scream, swinging my sword. *I won't let him touch a hair on her head—on any of their heads.*

Jeremiah blocks my attacks easily, and my arms are growing tired.

Glancing over my shoulder, I see Lia still at my back, fighting. "Where are the girls?" I shout over the clatter of swords.

Looking at Lia fight, you wouldn't know she was poisoned, like me. I guess she truly is the best warrior we have. "Cora has them," she pants as she swirls on her toe, swinging her axes and decapitating two men in one fluid motion.

Sharp pain laces through my thigh, dropping me to my knees. My sword falls from my grasp as I grip the wound. "I think I want to keep you around for a little while longer," Jeremiah muses.

Lia screams, and I turn just in time to see the man drive

his sword through her chest. One axe clashes with the blade as blood pools in her mouth. She takes one step forward, then another, driving the blade through her body and out the other side. The man looks on in shock; he doesn't see her swing her axe. It makes a sickening fleshy crunch as it meets the man's neck, not quite decapitating him. His head lands sickly as he falls to the ground.

"Lia..." I scramble towards her, where she falls to her knees. The blood is already slowing and her eyes are growing distant. "No, no, no! Look at me!" I shout, pulling the sword from her and tossing it aside. Her body falls lax in my arms.

She looks up, her eyes falling on the sky above. "Cyan," she coughs.

"I'm here. You're going to be okay."

Her brows pinch together. "Don't lie to me boy," she coughs again, her bloodied hand gripping the back of my neck. "You give them hell."

"Oh, how touching," Jeremiah chuckles. "But if you didn't notice, we're in the middle of a battle." His sword presses at Lia's throat.

"NO!" I shout, gripping the weapon in my hand. The metal slides through my grip, slicing open layer after layer of flesh and muscle. My teeth grind together. "NO!" I growl between them as the blade slides further through my grip and into Lia's throat.

"Oh, you act like you've never seen war before." Jeremiah grips my hair. "People die, and I'm going to make you watch it all!"

Something dull hits me in the back of my head, and everything goes black.

CHAPTER THIRTY-TWO
MALLRIE

Mother grips my arm, pulling me to a halt. Her eyes are wild as they search my face. "Promise me, Mallrie."

I shake my head. I cannot make that promise to her. The girls will be safe. I sent Cyan to take them straight to Cora's. She's got a wine cellar where they can hide. "I'm going to fight," I say matter-of-factly as I pull her arm off me. "I will not let Charleston destroy our family, our coven."

Mother's jaw tightens and she juts out her chin. Lifting a hand, mere sparks flare from her hand. "And how do you suppose you'll win, Mallrie, hm? The snake has poisoned our water. Our magic is..." Her voice trails off as she looks down at her hands. The High Witchess possesses a kernel of all elemental magic, and right now, she's trying to summon whatever she can. "This is Cyan's fault," she snaps. It causes me to pause from my activity of moving about our home, changing into my boots and finding weapons.

"What did you say?" Straightening up, I look down at where she's slumped into a chair, goblet of wine in hand. Our people are being *slaughtered* just beyond that door, and yet she sits here, drinking her fucking *wine* like it's any other Apus Day.

"You heard me." There's a venom in her tone that makes my spine stiffen. "That bastard has attracted the attention of a Nechkrappe. No doubt that foul creature has just been waiting for its curse to take effect and watch his downfall." Drinking deeply from her cup, she mutters, "Stupid boy."

"That's not what's happened," I comment, resuming my search for Cyan's blades. I noticed he didn't take them when he rushed the girls to Cora's. Panic floods me as I strap them to my hip. As soon as the vision faded of Charleston's hand pressing a distressed Hesper into the ground while he yanked feathers from her, I got Cyan to get our sisters to Cora and Lia's. To warn them of what's happened—what's going to happen. Cyan was beside himself with concern for Hesper. *"Get our sisters to Cora's and* then *go find Hesper,"* I told him. Stupid me didn't think to remind him to grab some weapons.

"No?" Our mother laughs. "You're more of a fool than I thought, then, which makes me glad I put off your ascension."

My teeth grind together at the reminder of her refusing to allow me to take my place as High Witch. I have spent the last month coming up with ways to improve our life in the coven, to incorporate Charleston and his people, utilise their skills and learn some of their customs.

Sheathing Cyan's blades at my side, I make my way to the door. "I will not let Charleston destroy my family or coven. High Witch or not, they're still my people, and I will protect them."

"Your family?" Mother scoffs, pushing to her feet and grabbing me by the strap of my sword across my chest.

"You won't have a family or a coven to ascend to and protect if you go out there without your magic."

I bare my teeth, once again forcing her to let go of me. "What an insult to all of Father's training then," I spit, watching her eyes widen at the mention of him. "Or didn't you know that he regularly used his magic to render my magic useless so I would be ready for it if this day ever came?"

The look on her face is priceless, and I wish Cyan was here to witness it. I won't mention what Atherton used to do to Cyan, knowing she wouldn't care either way.

"No," she breathes, her arms falling limply to her sides. "I never knew what he did in the forest with you."

"Then you know *nothing* of what he's put your sons through."

"Mallrie, wait!" She runs in front of me, placing her hands on my chest. "Don't do this, you'll *die*. Just—"

"Then an honourable death awaits me," I say, stopping her mid-speech.

"Now, you listen to me, boy!" She snatches the sword from my hand, glaring at me, and that small, scared boy with a baby thrust into his arms shivers inside me. "Let Leander and Lia lead the fight. You must protect your sisters and ensure the magic stays in Vaasis."

Snatching the sword from her grip and sliding it into the sheath along my back, I growl, "I will protect *all* of my family! Even your cold and hateful heart."

The sharp sting of her hand strikes my face. "Stupid boy," she spits between her teeth. "He is *not* your brother!"

I scoff, shaking my head and shaking off her cruel and meaningless words. She's just trying to hurt me.

"You..." Cersei breathes. When I turn to look at her

again, there's a sudden sense of clarity and shock spilled across her face. "You helped him murder your father."

I nod. Cersei swings her hand again, but this time I catch it, my thumb pressing into the tendons in her wrist. "And I would do it again in a heartbeat. *No child* should have to live in fear. And *no parent* should treat their child like you and Atherton treated Cyan," I spit at her feet, my lips curled back in disgust. With a firm push, Cersei stumbles back into her chair, tipping over the glass of wine. I don't bother to look at her again as I pick up the quiver of arrows and attach them to my thigh before retrieving the bow and notching an arrow in place. All the while, she just stands there, speechless.

"I made a promise that day to those scared boys. That I would let nothing hurt them." Shame creeps into my cheeks, and I have to look away from my mother's horrified face. "I had already failed Cyan." My knuckles turn white as I grip the bow. "I will not fail him again. Or my coven."

Turning my back on her, I head towards the front door, where the clash of metal and the screams of war are raging.

My mother calls behind me, "Do what you wish, you stubborn child, but promise me this: when they burn my body, you'll restore the magic to Vaasis. You'll restore peace to these lands. You'll make the ascension."

I stop in my tracks and slowly turn on my toe to face her. She stands there defiantly, her arms crossed over her chest and her chin held high. "What have you seen?" I ask.

"More than I should," she whispers, a look of regret on her face. "Promise me, Mallrie."

"I promise."

CHAPTER THIRTY-THREE

MALLRIE

Kneeling before Vaasis, blood and dirt press against my skin like a second skin, and the feeling of it makes me want to be physically sick. The first time I killed, Atherton was proud of me. I was proud of myself, but it was in self-defence. My mind would have been consumed by the juvenile meshlynk before it slaughtered me. The second time I killed, Atherton wanted to watch. Blood and dirt smeared across my skin and as I lay there next to the dead ashga, panting heavily. I wanted to rip my skin off. I hated the feeling of death on me. Atherton praised me and carried me on his shoulder home, the ashga's decapitated head in his hand like a trophy to show off to the coven. It was the first time I felt close to my father; killing an innocent creature brought us together. Bonded us somehow. And I *loathed* it.

I curl my fingers into fists to stop myself from trying to peel my skin away. *This is not who I want to be. I don't like what Atherton has turned me into.*

My head droops between my shoulders, unable to watch Charleston's people binding my coven to Vaasis or the bastardised pyres they've built on either side of the tree because far too many Enkantians stood with pride and didn't drop their knees to this tyrant. *I failed them, and I cannot even give them the honour of looking them in the eye in their final moments. What must they think of me? Mother was right. I'm not ready to become High Witch. I don't deserve the ascension when I wasn't able to save my people.*

Someone drops an unconscious body next to me and I try to rein in my flinch. Jeremiah has repeatedly dumped the dead next to me before moving them on, as if to antagonise me and showcase all that I've lost. All I can think about is how proud Atherton would have been to have a son like Jeremiah.

The body groans and my head snaps to the side to see Cyan lying in the dirt, bloody and bruised. The tension in my shoulders eases as I help him sit up. He groans out a long string of curses. "Are you okay?" I ask, grimacing at the stupidity of the question. He isn't okay. Nothing is okay.

Cyan just nods his head, still muttering curses about Jeremiah. A blood-curdling shriek has us turning our attention to where two men are hauling our sisters out of Cora and Lia's house. "NO!" I shout, pushing to my feet, but the wooden end of an axe crushes into my injured shoulder and I fall back into the bloody dirt, coughing and spitting a mouthful of blood.

"Leave them alone! *Please!*" I am not above begging at this point, and shameless tears blur my vision. Albert Charleston just stands beside Vaasis, a sneer on his face, as if enjoying this show. *"Please,"* I try again. "They're innocent. If you want to punish someone, take me."

My sisters are tossed on the ground before me, and Charleston chuckles darkly. "It's nice to hear you begging,

Mallrie Delacroix. Remember my mercy." He waves a hand, dismissing his men.

"Sir, there was another. She put up a fight," one of Charleston's men is saying as I grip Abeline's arm and pull her closer to me. Cyan is gathering Adriana and Alinta by his side, the former a sobbing mess in his arms and the latter sitting there frozen, a smear of blood across her face.

My blood runs cold as Charleston raises a brow, speaking with a coldness that even Atherton couldn't manage. "And what of her?"

"She's dead, sir. We killed her, but she managed to... *burn* Coleton. From the inside out."

Charleston waves a hand, unaffected and unfazed by this revelation. "Dump her body like the rest."

I cannot breathe. I cannot see anything other than Cora's lifeless body as it's dumped before me. Too much blood stains her simple cotton dress. Her eyes are open but not seeing anymore. A wail rips from my throat as I toss myself over her body, as if somehow I can stop them from taking her away.

"No, no, no, *NO!*" The word is a prayer spilling from my lips over and over. *"Please."* My voice breaks as a pair of boots stops before my line of sight. One of Charleston's men grabs Cora's arm and *pulls* her away from me. The sound of the bone popping out of the socket has me launching to my feet, jumping over her and pinning the man to the ground. My fist collides with his face, over and over and over. Flesh splits and bone eventually crumbles under my assault. I can feel people pulling at my shoulders, but I don't stop. My knees are locked in around his body. His teeth break, splitting open my knuckles in a painful slice that I ignore. I'd rather split my whole fucking hand open just so I can turn this man into an unrecognisable pulp of flesh and bloody matter.

I feel no remorse.

I feel *nothing*.

"That's enough," Charleston drawls, and something cracks into the side of my head, my vision blurring and fading.

Distantly, I feel hands grabbing me and pulling me away, but all I see is how they drag Cora's body away, tossing it into a mass grave just beyond the coven.

"It's time for change." Charleston's voice booms over the crowd. "Your High Witchess wouldn't see reason when it was presented to her. She didn't live up to these vows she swore. She didn't have your best interest at heart."

I kneel before Vaasis, looking forward to my mother, but not truly seeing her. I am nothing more than a shell, an empty husk of an Enkantian, kneeling before this tyrant who came into our lives only months ago and manipulated and poisoned us. Charleston's words bleed away. *Someone betrayed us.* I look at those tied to Vaasis, our sacred tree, and the stakes on either side. If they betrayed our coven, they wouldn't have been tied to those stakes, prepared to die. My eyes shift to the remaining Enkantians kneeling beside me. Abeline clings to my arm, sobbing loudly. Cyan and our other two sisters are on my other side. Selma is next to Abeline, her hand tracing soothing circles on her back as she bites back her tears. Her short blonde hair is streaked with blood, but her chin is held high, defiant against Charleston's words.

"The Enkanti Tree," his voice echoes through my head, snapping me out of my thoughts. "To remind you and our future generations of this day. Of the dangers of magic. Repeat it," Charleston demands. Abeline shudders a wet sob as the cool metal tip of a sword presses against the nape of her neck—the same kind as the ones pressing against mine and every other Enkantian kneeling before Charleston.

"The Enkanti Tree."

The words are repeated back in a mixture of sobs and defiant grits between clenched teeth. The words taste like ash on my tongue.

"Long live the king!" Charleston exclaims, followed by a chorus of his followers.

My body trembles as I search inside myself for a kernel of my magic to somehow make this right, even if it's just spilling Charleston's blood, but all I can manage is a loop of screams and the sensation of Cora's cold and stiff body beneath my hands. I look down at my hands, expecting to see her sightless eyes gazing back at me, but all that remains are flakes of blood and dirt.

Charleston continues to speak, as if he cannot get enough of the sound of his own voice. Maybe I'll rip out his vocal cords. *I know I should be listening intently to what he has to say to ensure the safety of my family, of what little remains of our coven. After all, they'll turn to me now.*

Standing next to the monster in mortal flesh is his black-hearted son, Jeremiah. His eyes are wholly on my broken-hearted sister. *I'll rip his eyes from their sockets, too. For all the times he looked at her with lust, and now, for looking down his nose at her as if she's inferior to him. Like she's worth nothing.*

A small red bud catches my eye as it pushes through the dirt and blood in front of me. Slowly, the bud shudders, unfurling into a begonia. My eyes slide to Cyan next to me, his fingers pressed deep within the earth. I rack my brain, trying to remember the meaning behind this flower, to decipher the message Cyan is trying to give me, but my mind is *hollow*. His forearm shudders, and I know it's taking every ounce of his strength to summon the wilting flower.

No tears line his dark eyes, just anger and vengeance as they find mine.

We hold each other's gaze, my arm tightening around Abeline's body for what is to come as a wave of searing heat hits the side of my face and an orchestra of screams erupts from Vaasis... the Enkanti Tree.

CHAPTER THIRTY-FOUR

MALLRIE

The embers around the base of Vaasis crackle softly as the first rays of dawn creep over the horizon. Charleston's people have long left, going to sift through the belongings of those they've slaughtered. The remaining handful of Enkantians return to their homes to mourn the loss of their families and of the life that they once knew quietly. Ashes fall like snow around Cyan and me, who are the last kneeling before the great tree that still stands, despite being consumed by flames and the screams of Enkantians for the last few hours. Flecks of ash collect on our clothes and in our hair. I watch our sisters, who are helping their friend Selma round up the witchlings and take them to Cora and Lia's. Alinta looks back at the tree, a golden glow haloing her dark hair. Her face is puffy from crying, and yet she holds a smile firmly in place as she scoops another witchling into her arms. A kid on each hip, I watch her walk over bloodied ground and discarded weapons.

The scarcity of the Enkantians left forms a knot of emotion in my throat.

There are twenty witchlings and five infants who survived. As for the mature elementals, I can count them on one hand. Avark Barre, Amos Langlais, Caspian Fournier and Zaelfe Charpentier. Along with Selma Beaumont, my sisters and Cyan. Ten witches left. The rest were slaughtered or burnt because they didn't drop their knee to Charleston.

Cyan and I had to force Abeline and Adriana to their knees to save them from joining our mother in her fate. My chest aches with burning questions. *Did we do the right thing? Would it have been more merciful to let them all burn and enter Vraska and the Afterlife rather than having to give up their magic and serve a man who is as cruel as he is cunning? What will happen to us if we do not use our magic?* My mind spins in circles of questions I do not have the answers to and planning how I can help what remains of the Enkantian Coven.

"I should have done more," I sigh, turning my attention away from the women taking the witchlings somewhere safe to eat, rest and mourn. The burnt corpses decorate the Enkanti Tree and the stakes set on either side of the great oak.

"There was nothing more you could have done," Cyan whispers beside me.

My hands curl into the dirt before me as my anger builds, the ash-covered dirt fragments of my people digging underneath my nails and seeping into my pores. "Surely, I could have done—"

"Mallrie, look at me," Cyan says, a snap of annoyance in his tone. "There is nothing you could have done. Don't beat yourself up over something you couldn't control."

My fist collides with the earth, sending the ashes that had settled on my shoulders and in my hair scattering to the ground. "I should have been able to protect my people," I hiss between clenched teeth. "Fuck what Avark says about looking into the *Timeline*. We should have been checking it to make sure we could trust Charleston. I had a bad feeling about him from the moment he stepped through the forest."

Cyan grips my elbow, pulling me to my feet. "Keep your voice down," he hisses, looking over his shoulder at the mortals taking claim of the homes of those they murdered. He drags me between the houses and into the forest, silencing me every time I open my mouth. Once we're deep enough in the treeline that he is satisfied we won't be over-heard, he turns to me and says, "It's in the past now. We cannot change it."

I look down at my hands. I can feel my magic slowly reawakening. Purple darkness speckled with tiny stars sparks from my palm. "I could try—"

Cyan grips my wrist, jerking it downwards. "Avark has told you never to go to the past. The consequences—"

"Fuck the consequences, Cyan. Our entire coven just got slaughtered! Cora and Lia..." That knot of emotion in my throat chokes the words from me, and I fall to my knees. Cyan told me of Lia's death. Hot tears burn my eyes as my forehead rests against the moss and dirt. It smells so fresh here, unlike the stench of death that stains what's left of our home.

Cyan kneels beside me, his hand awkwardly patting my shoulder in a disjointed rhythm. He stays with me while I mourn the loss of my family. Cora and Lia were more like parents to me than my own mother and father were. I've lost countless friends. The coven was like an extended family to me. Cyan never felt welcomed by them, yet he stays beside me.

The sky has turned dark and a blood moon hangs amongst the stars. Gazing at the red hue of the moon, I remember a rhyme my mother used to recite to me before bed. *"When the moon casts its eerie sheen, Fates entwine with threads unseen. The reaper's presence, an ethereal breath, a silent herald of impending death."*

For the longest time, I always thought the blood moon was a warning of death and destruction, but now it seems it's the Fates' way of reminding us that sometimes the monsters are inside us, thirsty for blood. I never wanted to be like Atherton. I never wanted to kill mercilessly. But that's what I did. It's what I've become. And I'd do it all again in a heartbeat.

"I'm going to restore the magic in Vaasis."

Cyan looks up at me from where he's sitting, his back resting against a tree, Hesper cradled in his lap. I can sense his worry. It's in the wide set of his eyes and the way his mouth opens and closes as he searches for the right words. Charleston made a promise to sentence anyone found using magic to death.

"I will protect my people, Cyan, whatever that takes."

"Are you going to make your ascension? You'll become the High Witch?" he asks quietly, as if afraid someone might overhear us.

I shake my head. "I don't know yet. I..." As I look around the forest, I can't help but notice the eerie stillness that seems to engulf every inch of it, almost as if every living creature—from the towering trees to the tiniest insects—is grieving the demise of the Enkantians. "I don't know if I deserve it."

"You do," Cyan says solemnly. "Don't force yourself into it. You'll know when the time is right."

I look from my dirty, blood-covered hands to Cyan. "Will I, though? How can I be fit to look after what's left of our coven when I couldn't protect them?"

Cyan shrugs a shoulder. "How did you know how to look after a baby when you were but a child yourself?"

"That was different," I breathe.

Cyan shakes his head. "Nah, I don't think so. I think you're far more capable now than you were then." A smile tugs at the corner of his mouth as he raises his hands. "Not that I'm saying you did a shit job. I think I'm fucking delightful."

I burst into laughter, shortly followed by Cyan's own. Amongst the death and sorrow, it feels good to laugh. To be thankful that my brother and sisters survived.

Our laughter subsides into mournful sighs as the weight of what's unfolded falls like a shroud around us once more.

"I will make things right, I promise," I voice the vow aloud—the last promise I made to Mother—letting my words and declaration be heard not just by Cyan but by the Fates as well.

"And Charleston will die," Cyan whispers, his voice dripping with vengeance and rage.

"And Charleston will die."

CHAPTER THIRTY-FIVE

CYAN

I've never feared Death. Her icy fingers were always within reach, slowly closing around my throat. Once again, I have evaded Death's grasp. Dodged every attack Charleston's men threw my way and coated my skin with their blood. I took their lives without remorse. With each swing of my blade and every neck I snapped, I eliminated some of the filth that plagued this world. Their screams still echo in my mind, and I will never forget the fear in their eyes as they met Death at my hands. It filled me with a rush that I hadn't felt since I dragged that cursed blade across Atherton's throat.

I've never feared death. When you walk alongside it long enough, you make friends with the inevitable.

Everyone will die, even you.

Mallrie and I drank what was left of the good whisky in Erik's cellar when we returned to the coven—or what remained of it. Though the homes and buildings still stand, there is a sense of loss in the air.

I left Mallrie to stew in his grief and self-loathing. I walked away from his hateful words and what was left of the Enkantian Coven and out into the cold and quiet night. Our sisters took the witchlings to Cora and Lia's along with their friend, Selma Beaumont, a wretched little witch who could have burned with the rest of the coven, and I wouldn't have cared. My sisters see something in her I cannot.

The magic in Vaasis is already waning. *I wonder what Charleston will demand we call it now? I can't imagine he'd like us to keep referring to it as something that has ties to magic.* The insatiable clicking sounds of the Kailadons that lurk within the forest are closer than they've ever been. Nevertheless, I head into the treeline. I don't fear the Kailadons or whatever other creatures dare to lie in wait in the shadows. There is only one man-eating creature I am in search of tonight.

"Oh, for the sake of what's left of my sanity, please stop with the melodramatic monologue, Cyan!" Hesper screeches into my mind.

I look to the trees and find her perched high on a branch, her foot on the carcass of something I'd rather not look at too closely as her sharp beak rips off a piece of flesh. "You're more than welcome to stay out of my head," I remind her, making a conscious effort not to walk under the tree she's in.

"You think so loudly, though, that sometimes it's hard."

My teeth grind together. "Was it hard for you to assist Charleston in poisoning my people? Poisoning me?"

Hesper hisses, a black shadow swooping over me. I try not to flinch as the wind from her wings brushes against the top of my head. The Nechkrappe lands with grace, wings outstretched, a coil of dark magic rolling off them. *"I did not betray you, Cyan,"* she hisses. *"How many more times must I tell you?"*

My eyes narrow as I take in her large wingspan and milky eyes. "How else did Charleston know how to restrict our magic? You gave me a feather to do the same to Atherton." I step around her, my boot gently knocking one of her wings aside. "What else am I meant to think?"

Hesper scoffs. *"There's more than one way to skin a cat, Cyan. Do you think the Enkantians are so powerful that only the feather of a Nechkrappe can restrict their magic?"*

The blood moon washes the water in its sinister glow. Stripping my clothes and boots, I make my way into the water. A familiar figure shimmers just beneath the surface. "Hello, Az," I drawl as a pair of eyes look up at me.

"Hello, Cyan," the mermaid almost sheepishly replies. Her skin shimmers under the moon's glow, her hair falling naturally around her as if it doesn't abide by the same rules as everyone else's when they just resurface from the lake. "Since when do you venture this deep into the forest after dark?" Her hands trail up my bare legs as I sit on the lake's edge in my undershorts.

"Everyone's dead," I breathe, the words stinging my throat. Shame clings to my body like an extra skin for sneaking off in the middle of the night while Mallrie is left to... well, look after everything else. With the High Witchess' passing, they'll all turn to him now. Whether he makes the ascension, he will be the High Witch, and if Charleston had known that, he would have tied Mallrie to that tree along with our mother. His life is in danger, and here I am, selfishly running away to seek comfort for the massacre of my mother and coven, who wouldn't think twice if they saw me fall on that battlefield, or tied to Vaasis or one of the stakes and burnt alive.

Azalea smiles and splashes me playfully with her tail, snapping me out of my thoughts. "I said, that must feel like a relief."

My brows press together. "Surprisingly, no."

"No?" Her voice pitches higher, and her hands grip my hips and pull me into the water. "And why would that be?" Her hands slip around my neck, and holding me close, I can feel her powerful tail swishing below the water, keeping us in place.

My scowl deepens as I ponder her question. "I worry about Mallrie," I finally answer. "I fear Charleston will find out that he's the one the coven will turn to now, and murder him. I fear for my sisters..."

"So, you do not mourn the dead?" Az interrupts.

I roll my lips into my mouth, trying to understand this feeling swirling around in my chest. "No," I breathe. "Mallrie lost a lot of friends, lovers and family. And as kind as some of them tried to be, I could always sense their apprehension around me. So, no, I don't mourn them. I mourn for Mallrie and my sisters, and the losses they feel."

Azalea's hands are roaming over my body. "Maybe we should celebrate then?" Her smile is all sinister beauty. "The fall of the great Enkantians," she chuckles. "Mishk."

My brows furrow. I'm not familiar with that word. Az pulls herself closer, her breasts pressing against my skin as her lips trail along the shell of my ear, causing me to shudder. "Beautiful but deadly." Pulling away, she shrugs. "Or so it's been roughly translated. Deadly," another shrug of the shoulder, "tragic. It's all the same."

"La mort est la mort," I reply.

"Exactly."

Azalea pulls me under the water's surface, her lips pressing against mine in a desperate kiss. I don't pull away. Instead, I move my hand down her body and squeeze her breast, rolling her hardened nipple under my thumb.

I can hear Az's muffled moans as I move on to kissing her neck. With every kiss, my body screams for more while my lungs burn from the loss of precious air. I hold out a little longer, enjoying the pain with the pleasure I know Az is feeling under my careful kisses and kneading hands.

The night's cool air caresses my skin, and I take a truly needed breath, but Azalea doesn't break the surface with me. Instead, her hands trail down my body and slip my undershorts from me before her warm mouth wraps around my cock.

Azalea moves me through the water until I am sitting on a rock, the water still around my chest and her lips around my cock. The water ripples where her head is bobbing just below the surface. A shudder works its way down my spine, and I twist my fingers into her long blonde hair and pull her off. A pair of eyes and fin-like ears appear out of the water. She raises an eyebrow in silent question.

"If you're going to make me cum, I'm going to cum in that tight little slit of yours."

Azalea lifts herself out of the water, her hands pressing on the rock on either side of me and her breasts pressing against my chest. "How do you want me, Cyan?"

My hand snaps out and grips the back of her neck to stop her from retreating. "You're perfect just the way you are, Az," I murmur, my lips inches from her own.

She shivers in my grip. "As are you, Cyan," she whispers, her tongue darting out and caressing my lips. "Never forget it."

I scoff. Everyone in my life has always told me I was a mistake, a problem, a blemish on our family's image. Azalea is the only one to ever see me as a person, a life.

"How long can you hold your breath?" she asks, pulling me off the rock and into the water. "Will you cum before you drown?"

Sucking a lungful of air in, I dip below the surface and swim to the bottom of the lake. The water churns around me as Azalea stalks and swims in circles. *Show off.* Her hands grip my shoulders and spin me so I face the surface far above me. The blood moon glistens on the ripples of the surface. Az's hand grabs my cock and works my length a few times. I grip her tail and pull her closer, squeezing tightly where her ass would be. My other hand drags from her breast down her stomach to her slit, perfectly camou-flaged between her scales. Pressing two fingers inside, the little suckers latch onto me as I pump my fingers inside her.

Azalea tilts her head back, bubbles escaping her gaping mouth as she moans. Curling my fingers, I have her on the brink of her orgasm. Her hand snaps down to my wrist before she cums and pulls my hand free. Lifting my hand, she wraps her mouth around my fingers, sucking them deeply, tasting herself on them. Mermaids have an incred-ible sense of taste, but I guess that's needed when you live in the water. It has always made me wonder how much they can taste. But I don't have time to wonder about such depraved things as Az guides my cock into her warm slit. Her suckers grip and pull me in, and it's a fight to keep my mouth shut and not to moan at the sensation.

My lungs are burning from the lack of oxygen and my body is already fighting to swim to the surface, but Az pins me to the lake floor. She can lend me some air, but she'll only do that if I am on the brink of death. Little Siren is a sadist. Instead, I focus on keeping my heart rate even and letting out only small bits of air at a time.

Azalea's smile is purely sinful as she drags herself off my cock before driving herself back down. I shake my head, a smirk tugging at the corners of my lips as I grip her hips and force her down harder. Faster.

Azalea's head flings back, and a scream of pure ecstasy ruptures from her.

Fuck the air. With her neck exposed like that, I waste no opportunity to move my hands, wrapping them around her back and bringing her sweet and earthy skin to my lips. My teeth sink into the soft and delicate flesh, and I can feel the suckers inside Az shudder and squeeze my cock tighter and... *fuck*. It's a miracle from the Fates that I don't cum right here and now.

My head is aching, and my vision is fading out with the lack of oxygen. I tap Az's tail twice, our sign that I am about to pass out, and her lips press against mine. My lungs expand with a breath that has my head spinning.

"You're doing so fucking good, baby." Az's sweet words of praise mingle with the sensation of her tight grip on my balls, causing an involuntary moan to escape my lips and precious air.

My release creeps up my spine. Azalea's laughter is my favourite sound in the world, and it flitters around me before she presses her lips to mine again, stealing my breath this time instead of helping me. She squeezes my balls again, and I curse into her mouth as my orgasm rushes through me.

Azalea and I lay on the grassy bank, watching the sunrise. She slept for a few hours, but she mainly stayed awake to listen to me ramble about all the ways life is going to change now that the Enkantians are practically extinct.

"Should you be returning?" she asks quietly. "Will you return?"

I roll onto my back, looking at the sky shift from dark blue to purple to pink. "Not today."

"Why?" I can imagine the arch of her brow and the quirk of her lips that always appears when she's prodding me for information I'd rather leave unsaid.

Sighing, I tell her the truth. Not just because I trust her, but because I'm too damn tired to listen to her begging for answers. Even though she does the most wonderful things when she begs. "Because Mallrie and I fought before I left."

"About what?"

"What do you think?" I scoff, sitting up and resting my elbows on my knees. "He blamed me for Charleston figuring out how to poison the coven."

"You... you didn't, did you?" Az asks, and my head spins in her direction so fast, I feel a muscle spasm. "I'm just saying," she continues with a small shrug, "you've never really been on good terms with your coven. I'm sure no one would blame—"

"*No,*" I growl. "I didn't *poison* my coven. Despite everything, I'd never do that to them."

Azalea holds her hands up. "Just checking."

We sit in silence, watching the sky change colours. "I'm

sure Mallrie didn't *actually* think you had anything to do with it. If I was to take a stab in the dark, I'd say your mother had whispered in his ear something about it."

I look at her but say nothing because she could be right. The mer have ways of knowing more than they ever let on.

Az lifts a shoulder, her long blonde hair falling away. "He loves you, Cyan. That man raised you from a baby when he was a witchling himself. That type of loyalty and love doesn't just disappear."

Dropping my face into my hands, I press my fingers into my eyes until bursts of colours appear. "I know, but it's... I just need time." I turn to look at Az. My throat feels like it's burning behind the knot there. "Besides, I don't think I'll be able to see you as much anymore. Not with Charleston keeping such a close eye on us. It's... it's probably best if this is goodbye."

CHAPTER THIRTY-SIX

MALLRIE

"Don't you fucking *touch* them!" My voice is hoarse and broken as I struggle to push Charleston's people away from where they've half-heartedly discarded my sisters' bodies.

One of the men scoffs and mutters some perverse insult. Cyan's hands barely catch my shirt before I get that man by the throat, squeezing until his pathetic face turns red, then purple. There's an uproar around me, but all I can hear is their screams, begging for their lives. The witchlings cried as Charleston's people brutally murdered them. I drop the man, who gasps for air, but before he can regain himself, my fingers are deep within his eye sockets, ripping them out and shoving them down his throat. His screams become a gurgle as he chokes on his eyeballs.

Something sharp pierces my side and I can distantly hear Cyan shouting, then pleading. I roll onto my back and look up at the sky.

Everything doesn't seem as bright as it once was.

Cyan is bargaining with Charleston. The words are a distant rumble as I place my hand at my side, feeling the sticky blood oozing from the wound. My magic—which I swore never to use again—hums in my blood, seeking to slow time, slow the bleeding. *Fuck Charleston and everyone else.* I allow time to slow just around the wound. It's such an insignificant amount of magic that no one will notice. *No one is left to notice.*

None of the remaining Enkantians came out today to watch Charleston slaughter the witchlings and our sisters. They didn't bother to stop him. To scream, plead and beg for mercy. Selma was there for the briefest of moments before turning to Jeremiah, claiming another wave of morning sickness. More like she didn't want to see her friends step up to the beheading stone.

Even Alinta, knowing what her fate was to be, was still trying to bargain with the power-hungry bastard for the witchlings' safety.

"Take him away and keep him out of my sight!" I hear Charleston grumble.

"Of course, sir. Thank you." Cyan's grovelling makes me sick, hearing that timid voice once more. His boot hits me right in the fucking side. I stifle a curse as he bends down and mutters, "You fucking moron. Are you trying to get yourself killed, too?"

Fury pumps through my blood, and if it weren't for Atherton's ruthless years of training, there'd be a lot more blood spilt today. *Patience,* I remind myself, knowing that if we attack now, we too will lose our lives. Not that they overly seem to matter anymore, now that Charleston has murdered our sisters and the witchlings, but they deserve vengeance. And there are still the *other* Enkantians still alive, even though they are just as bad as Charleston and his people in my mind. Selma stood by Jeremiah's side, her stomach starting to swell with his child—the only reason she wasn't under the Enkanti Tree and her head on the chopping block.

"Like with Father?"

This is the first time Cyan hasn't spoken to me with hostility or silent loathing in months, and it draws me out of my thoughts as we sit a healthy distance apart under the shade of the Enkanti Tree. I didn't handle things very well when the flames became nothing more than embers after Charleston burnt our mother and the majority of the coven. Fear and anger coursed through my veins as I made sure the rest of our coven was safe and had whatever I could provide them with. All the while, Cersei's words rang too loudly in my mind, sowing seeds of doubt.

"It's your fault that they're all dead!" I shout as I pushed him back towards the door. Adriana's hands fist in my shirt, pulling me away from Cyan, pleading with me to stop. "Why do you think we've sung warnings about them? They're dangerous, loathing creatures who don't give a fuck about anything or anyone but themselves!"

"Hesper had nothing—"

"YES, it did! It doesn't have a soul, Cyan! It doesn't care about you. It's using you like a fool!"

"You don't know what the fuck you're talking about!" Cyan pushes back, and Adriana stumbles to the floor. He curses under his breath as he tries to step around me to help her.

"I think you've done enough, Cyan," I say, stepping in his way. *"Do you truly hate us enough to want to kill us all?"*

His green eyes shift to me. His dark brows arch with the hurt my words slice through him. "I had nothing to do with this, nor Hesper. You..."

I scoff. "There are only two possibilities of how Charleston could have poisoned us like he did. One of the ways, only you and I know. The other would require a powerful earth elemental." I arch a brow in his direction, the accusation lingering unspoken between us.

"...you can ask her yourself." Cyan's voice drops to barely a whisper.

"And how do you expect I do that?"

Cyan never answered me, his cheeks flushed with embarrassment and his eyes dropped to the floor.

He left after that. Cyan just *left* and didn't return for two days. I was afraid he would not return. *Why would he after he just got free of Atherton's iron fist only to be caught in Charleston's? Why would he return after I said such hateful and hurtful words?*

For two days, I sat by the door waiting for his return, mulling over our fight and regretting it all.

Weeks later, the tension is still thick in the air, even as the summer breeze shifts through the leaves of the Enkanti Tree. I look down at my hands, at the stones that now lay where grass and dirt once were.

"He doesn't hold your anger against you," a sultry female voice slithers into my mind, causing me to flinch and look up into the branches of Vaasis. *The Enkanti Tree,* I mentally correct myself. Then I find Hesper. Her neck is twisted at an

odd angle as she nibbles at her wing. *"He still cares, just... give him time."*

I roll my eyes. It took Cyan another two weeks until he came to me, Hesper perched on his shoulder, and she spoke into my mind for the first time. The guilt that crashed over me was all-consuming.

Cyan looks at me, his fingers laced together as he leans forward, resting his forearms on his bent knees, waiting for my response. I nod, my face twisted into what my sisters feared would be a permanent scowl after *"the Fall of the Witches,"* as Charleston proclaimed.

Their fear has become a reality.

I doubt I'll find much happiness in this world now that Charleston has ripped them from me. I can still feel the spray of their blood on my skin as I knelt before them, screaming and begging him to spare them and the other witchlings while a sword was pressed to Cyan's and my throats. His fear and greed for power and dominance poisoned him. No child was to survive because of his irrational fear that they would rise against him.

"Like with Father," I repeat. Neither of us need to say more. I don't need Cyan's help, and honestly, the less blood on his soul, the better. But I feel this is something he'll want to be involved in.

Revenge.

CHAPTER THIRTY-SEVEN

MALLRIE

Night comes, but the sticky, unforgiving heat doesn't diminish with the fall of the sun. Cyan and I sit in our too-empty, too-quiet home that isn't our own. Charleston took that from us too, not that I minded. I would gladly sacrifice all of our worldly belongings to ensure the safety of our sisters. But nothing could have protected them from his fear. The whisky burns my throat. Charleston's people don't know how to brew a smooth blend like Erik could. Maybe it was his magic that helped. Maybe he was just more gifted than Charleston's people.

Winifred is curled up in my lap, purring softly. Her hind legs hang off me and her front paws dangle over the arm of the chair. She's becoming too large to still be resting on top of me, but after everything we've been through, I just want to keep her close. I run my fingers over her head and between her horns, her four eyes half-lidded with the pleasure of my pets.

I can't bring myself to throw away the broken bottle from Erik's tavern that I am clutching in my hand. Winnie found it a few days ago when I took her out to hunt. It looked like someone had smashed it against a tree near the forest. Too many good memories are in that hall. Taking Cyan there for the first time, how we drank and laughed like there were no secrets between us, like we had not a worry in the world. My magic flares in my veins, and music and laughter ring in my ears. I can see our sisters dancing on the tabletops and singing at the top of their lungs, slightly off-tune.

Now we sit in silence—or near silence. The sound of the Kailadons that now stalk through the town Charleston is trying to build on the bones of our coven. The muffled sounds of children crying in fear of the creatures outside their homes, their mothers trying in vain to settle them into their beds for the night.

"There was nothing I could do, Cyan," I say, breaking the silence between us.

His eyes, a darker shade than mine but still eerily similar, flick up to me. "What is the good of being a time elemental if you cannot go back in time?" he seethes. "Seems like a pretty fucking useless magic to have if you ask me." He takes a sip of his amber-coloured whisky and I have to bite my tongue to stop myself from snapping back.

What a change of tune you've had, brother, I think sombrely. Only a month ago, he was the voice of reason, stopping me from using my magic to go back in time and stop Charleston.

"And yet you were celebrated," Cyan snarls over his glass. "Adored. Because of your magic." He spits the words with such disdain and hatred that he reminds me of our father.

I close my eyes and focus on calming myself. My magic is thrumming erratically beneath my skin like it has every day since Charleston murdered the witchlings and our sisters.

"I told you. I did," I say slowly through gritted teeth. "Despite Avark's warnings. *Your* warnings." My voice trembles with emotion and the sickly feeling of looking back and forth through the *Timeline,* searching for something I could have done differently. "No matter what, the Fates..." my voice trails off as I remember the hundreds of ways I have witnessed my sisters being brutally murdered.

Neither of us says another word until it's time to leave.

To murder Charleston.

His will be slow and painful at the hands of a Kailadon, unlike our father, who had a relatively quick death, even if his soul is forever trapped in Cyan's blade.

CHAPTER THIRTY-EIGHT

CYAN

In the dark of night, as everyone cowers away in their stolen homes, Mallrie and I cover ourselves with dark cloaks, concealing weapons and stepping into the monster-filled night. The Kailadons aren't the only monsters that lurk in the dark. Monsters come in all shapes and sizes. They're disguised as beautiful, trumpet-shaped flowers, friendly smiles and olive tree branches shared between new friends. Looking around, Charleston has, in such a short period, changed so much of our home. Some houses are in the process of being torn down and rebuilt with stronger materials. They're also a lot larger than the humble Enkantian homes.

A guttural clicking sounds from behind us and I spin on my toe, pulling my sword from its sheath ready for the attack. "It's okay," Mallrie says, placing a hand on my shoulder. I almost flinch at the contact. His hand glows a subtle purple, and small stars and constellations float around the purple mist.

"You're using your magic?" I ask, surprised.

Mallrie slides his eyes to meet mine. "What do I have to

lose?" he asks, and the hurt in his voice lands like a physical blow.

What do *we have to lose? Everything we've ever cared for is gone. Charleston has destroyed our family, our home and our identity.*

I shrug a shoulder, feigning nonchalance. "You made a promise," I say. "And a Delacroix *always* keeps their promises." My eyes roll as I recite what Atherton drilled into us.

"What good is keeping a promise when it no longer benefits those you love?" Mallrie stops walking, his hands dropping to his side, but the magic stays firm. "When those you swore to are no longer here?" *He must be going near crazy with all his pent-up magic.* "You hardly want to even look at me, and when you do, you look at me as if I'm *him*. I tried *everything* I could to save the girls. The coven. And yet—"

"So much for being great and powerful *time elementals,*" I sneer. "Maybe we all should have been pitying you and Avark for your useless magic instead of revealing it?"

Mallrie humphs and shakes his head, not daring to look at me. "Is this the conversation you want to have right now?"

"Another time then." I smile smugly at him.

Mallrie looks like he would like to say something else, but holds his tongue. The magic swirling around his hands wanes, and I wonder if he's doing that on purpose to make his point or if using his magic is draining. I've found that when I've snuck deep into the forest because my magic feels like ants crawling under my skin, even the simplest of spells have left me feeling exhausted. Az tells me that using magic is like a muscle. The more you use it, the easier it is, but when you don't use it for extended periods, it becomes laborious. But I do remember the times I'd follow Mallrie into the forest late at night when the magic in the Enkanti

Tree finally dwindled away and the Kailadons started to prowl the streets. He'd sneak into the forest, use his magic to create a ward that not even I could penetrate, and then he'd slip between Time.

The first time he did it, I almost broke my fucking hand trying to get through the wards to get to him. Panic ripped away all my common sense and all I knew was I had to get to him. When he came back into his body, I saw the devastation on his face. The look of horror as he must have witnessed our sisters' deaths over and over and over. Yet, that didn't stop him from continuing to try.

It doesn't take long for us to make it to our old home by the large oak tree that sits dormant without magic flowing through her roots and branches. Our home is almost unrecognisable with the changes Charleston demanded, yet there's a familiar glow seeping through the cracks of the wooden slats, closed and latched from the inside to keep the Kailadons and other predators away.

"How would you like to do this?" Mallrie asks. The question comes as a surprise, and I find myself blinking at him, speechless. He shrugs. "I just assumed since you don't trust me, you'd want to take point." He nods to our former home, where the man who took everything from us sleeps peacefully inside.

My brows pinch together, and my mouth feels dry. "I do trust you." The words come out in a breathless whisper. "I'm just..."

"Grieving?"

I nod, trying to force the burning knot in my throat to fuck off.

My eyes sting as Mallrie claps a hand on my shoulder. His expression shifts from cocky to sympathetic, and I think that's worse when he says, "It's okay to be hurt. Everyone grieves in their own way." I step back, brushing his hand from me. "It's okay, Cyan. You're allowed to be angry. You're allowed to be angry at me."

My hands ball into fists at my sides. "Just stop, okay?" The tears are dangerously close. They're rimming my lash line, causing my vision to blur. "Stop being so... empathetic. So understanding. Just let me be angry. Let me—"

"Push away the last person who still cares about you?"

"Yes!" I hiss. It's too painful to be around him. To have him let me lash out with my sharp words, trying push him away. He's just a constant reminder of all that we've lost. Of the pain and grief that he carries on his shoulders. Pain and grief that he'll never be able to shake, because he'll never be able to forgive himself.

"A Delacroix always keeps their promise," Mallrie scoffs, shaking his head. "I made a promise when I first held you that I would always love you. There's nothing you can do that will break this bond."

"Why do you care? So many did not."

Mallrie smiles. It's a little lopsided, and in the dim light of the moon, I can see the small scar through his lip. "Because no matter what, you're my brother."

Something in my chest loosens at his words. "Then let's go kill this motherfucker."

CHAPTER THIRTY-NINE

MALLRIE

1985

Winifred leaps off the small porch, her enormous paws sinking into the snow as she lands. A keening sound vibrates in the back of her throat as she rubs a paw over her hornless head. Only two ember eyes blink up at me, and a stone of guilt settles in my chest, knowing she's absorbed her horns and extra eyes to attempt to blend in. "Sorry, Winnie," I say, stroking her spotted coat. "Not today." The large misnac hisses at me before shaking out her head and blinking her extra set of eyes. "Don't start," I say, pointing a finger towards the house where there are large claw marks on the glass panels that I just replaced. "You know you can't come into the town, no matter how well you disguise yourself. I won't risk it. Neither will Cyan."

Winnie flicks her forked tongue out at me before trotting off in search of Cyan. I check the small watch on my wrist as I follow her large footprints in the snow. Around the back of the small stone house Cyan and I built deep within the Melsheim Forest, I find my brother kneeling, the sleeves of his shirt rolled up as he tends to the small aeimweriah. "Have I killed anything?" I ask, leaning against the chilly stone wall with my arms folded across my chest.

Cyan scoffs, not bothering to look up at me. "Almost, but nothing I can't fix." It's nice to see him in his element again.

A smile tugs at my lips, and though I already know his answer, I ask anyway, just to see the annoyance build on his shoulders. "Can I help?"

Cyan snorts. "Absolutely not." His eyes meet mine and we smile at each other, at the memory of the last time I tried to help him tend to the small memorial to our sisters, our coven. I mistook a plant for a weed and pulled out an entire row before Cyan realised. Needless to say, I was promptly removed from the garden and strictly instructed on how to care for the vegetable patch. Apparently, they're a lot sturdier than the flowers in the aeimweriah.

"There," Cyan says, straightening and dusting the dirt and snow from his pants. "I really hate leaving." He looks longingly at the garden. It doesn't look like much now in the height of winter, but come spring, it'll be blooming once again with vibrant colours. Cyan's gaze drifts away from the aeimweriah around the rest of the yard, at the small slice of the Melsheim Forest that we carved out and made our own all that time ago.

Winnie presses her large body up against Cyan's side, her tail wrapping around his thigh, a silent plea not to leave. He smiles, patting her head and clicking his tongue playfully. "What are these?" he says, tugging on one of Winnie's curved horns, all semblance of her trying to blend in now gone. The misnac hisses at him, trying to get out of his grip. Cyan smooshes her face together. "Isn't Mallrie telling you all about the big, bad men who'll kill you if you're different?" His laughter has a rough edge to it. It sounds almost cruel, not like the laugh he used to have.

"Leave her be, Cyan," I say, stepping forward and pulling Winnie out of his grip. "She's safe in here. The wards will protect her."

"I'm just having a laugh," Cyan says, but there's no hint of humour on his face. "Or have you forgotten what that feels like?"

Some days I feel like I have. Like there's nothing left inside me but sorrow and regret. How can I feel joy or laughter when I've failed my family, my coven?

"Don't worry," Cyan says, waving his hand as if to dismiss the awkward tension building. "I know you're eating yourself with the guilt of everything that's happened. No one is going to get through those wards unless you want them to." His face turns serious, and his voice drops. "I know you're trying your best. She's safe."

I nod once, a subtle dip of my chin as I think. *If only I could say the same about you.*

We walk in silence across the extensive field that stretches between the Melsheim Forest and the town of Datura. The buildings stretch five stories into the sky, their rich red brick facades stained with grime that the townsfolk don't look too closely at. They ignore the fact that blood clings to the buildings as much as the dirt. They ignore the fact that their buildings stack on top of one another, leaving little room for wagons (not that they use them much anymore)

to get through. Charleston and his heirs, too afraid to take more than they already have, boxed the people of Datura in a small, circular box. It doesn't give the people much space to breathe anything other than the stench that clings to the stone like a veil. It's subtle, and I don't think the townsfolk realise how rotten their town smells without the magic. The Kailadons roam the streets of Datura, consuming any living thing they stumble upon, the stench of death and decay clinging to the stone the townsfolk walk upon.

"Stop fidgeting," Cyan hisses as we step off the grass and my shoes click against the paved path. His hand finds mine and tugs it away from this infernal wristwatch.

"It's too tight," I say as I loosen the band.

"It's meant to be tight," Cyan replies, slapping my hand away once more. "Otherwise it'll slip around, and you'll look like an idiot."

"Why do you insist I wear it?" I sigh, defeated, and drop my hands to my sides, but not before I give my right wrist a good shake.

"So you know the time, you big dummy."

I open my mouth to snap back a comment, but we both know why we wear these infuriatingly tight watches—so if we split up, we can arrange a time and place to meet back before I return to the forest. Not a plan I was happy with when Cyan suggested it, but one that I go along with, anyway.

I can't help but smirk as we pass one of the doorways, an arched window above the door frame, runes carved into the woodwork by their holy men who pray to fake gods. It's a sham, and yet the townsfolk believe these scribbles will protect them from the Kailadons. A labyrinth of burnt clay brick sucks me in as we walk through the meandering and senseless alleyways that all lead to the heart of Datura—to the Enkanti Tree.

Vaasis, my mind whispers to me. The Enkantian word almost sounds foreign after all these years. It feels like all the air is being sucked from my lungs, and my head spins like it does every time I enter the town. My magic presses painfully close to the surface, and I can hear their screams.

Straightening my shoulders, I take a deep breath. The stale air fills my lungs as I remind myself, *you're the rock when the storm comes*. My magic fades as we push through the crowds of people filling their day before they lock themselves away in their homes before the sun sets.

Charleston's blood still runs through the veins of this newly elected mayor. "What is his name again?" I whisper to Cyan, who lights up a cigarette.

He tilts his head back, his long blonde hair falling over his shoulder as he blows out that first breath. "Edgar McQuoid."

I grunt my acknowledgement and Cyan continues rattling off facts he's learnt about McQuoid since he started working in the General Disciplinary Office. Only a few facts land: he's got a son who works with Cyan, his wife passed away a few months ago, and he's friendly with a woman who owns a small cafe in the heart of town—a rarity, Cyan says, but I don't listen to why. I detest coming into this town and seeing the oak tree in its centre, no longer a symbol of our union with the Fae or safety. No, every time I see that Fates-forsaken tree, all I see are my failures. My family, friends and coven were lost at the hands of a scared and intimidated man.

A familiar black shadow flies over us, and I look up to see where Hesper has gone, but she's disappeared as if she was never there to begin with. I feel for Winnie, being left behind when Hesper can seemingly fly wherever she pleases.

"He's a slippery fucker, that's for sure. I caught him leaving the library just before curfew." Cyan snorts. "Well, they don't enforce the curfew, even though I've suggested it a dozen times. Edgar wants the people to have some semblance of freedom. But they all know to be inside before nightfall."

"What are you rambling about?" I ask, rubbing my eyes with my thumb and forefinger. I can already feel a headache building, and though this reminds me of a better time when Cyan was passionate about his studies, it also makes me sad.

"Edgar—well, Edgar Junior. Why do they both have to have the same name? These people don't make it easy." Cyan's still rambling. "Young McQuoid is reading through the old journals. You know, the ones Charleston was obsessed with keeping, and then Jeremiah decided to keep the dumb tradition alive." He winks at me as he knocks into a man walking the opposite way. They quickly apologise to each other, and as Cyan turns his attention back to me, he holds out the newspaper he slipped from the crook of the man's elbow.

I raise an eyebrow at the clever little tricks he's picked up spending time in Datura, but Cyan ignores it as he taps on the headline.

Can the Past be the Key to Our Future? By Edgar McQuoid.

"It appears old Junior has been moonlighting at the Datura Chronicles. I don't know how old daddy feels about it, but he's got enough people in his pocket that I guess he can do whatever he wants."

Skimming the text, I'm grateful that Cyan and I went through all of Charleston's and Jeremiah's incessant ramblings and ripped out any information about the Enkantians. Cyan's been continuing our tradition. If one of the mayors stumbles upon something, he's there to scrub it clean. We don't need the townsfolk finding out that there's dormant magic here. Not yet at least.

We sit on our usual bench in the centre of the township of Datura, looking into the Enkanti Tree. I cross one leg over the other and try to blend in with this new millennial crowd. I fidget with the timepiece on my wrist again.

"Leave it alone," Cyan chides from beside me as he flicks the newspaper to make the ridiculously large pages stand straight. "You'll draw unwanted attention."

I end up unstrapping the stupid thing and tossing it in a nearby trash can. It feels too tight on my wrist; the clasp presses into my veins and I can feel the thrum of my magic unnervingly close to the surface.

Cyan clicks his tongue in disapproval. "Get that out," he reprimands, glaring at me from the corner of his eye.

"What is the point?" I ask.

What is the point of any of this? Cyan agreed when I suggested we freeze our *Timelines*, stopping us from ageing so that we can fulfil the promises we've made. Though I physically haven't aged, I am tired. Watching the years go by has become tedious, and I am over protecting the people of Datura, whose parentage dates back to some of the worst days of my life.

"The point," Cyan starts with a sigh, "is that it was a very expensive watch."

I roll my eyes. He has enjoyed watching as the people of Datura grow and adapt. With the changing fashion and trends, he's always been at the forefront, getting the most expensive and ridiculous items. Like that idiotic timepiece they call a watch, which is stupid and makes no sense.

"I'm sure I can pay you back, brother," I remark. After all, we have more money than we need, having accumulated some wealth over the years working odd jobs when we wanted to be closer to the town than just coming at night. Living in a town infested with flesh-eating monsters means the townspeople stick to themselves and their closest connections. Which means, thankfully, we go unnoticed.

Yet with all the money we've obtained over the years, Cyan still has a penchant for stealing a few of these luxurious items. It doesn't bother me anymore. After all, these people took something that could never be replaced.

Our family.

CHAPTER FORTY
MALLRIE

Cyan splits the newspaper and hands half to me. We sit in silence as I watch the people of Datura mill about from over the rim of the paper, some setting up for the Spring Equinox. A celebration *we* taught Charleston. It is a time to celebrate the coming of life out of the harsh winter season. Now, it's just a commercialised shindig, no rituals or prayers held except to the Gods Charleston and his ever so precious *Crown* on the other side of the Melsheim Forest believed in. I return my attention to the paper in hand to distract myself and my anger with the trivial gossip that's newsworthy.

"Hello, Cyan," a melodic female voice says, filled with warmth. I flip through my newspaper, which has surprisingly captured my attention with an article about the agricultural development of tomatoes. My eyes slide to Cyan to see the colour creeping across his cheeks as Morana stands before him. She's a beautiful woman, with rich, olive skin and green eyes framed by a curtain of dark hair. She shifts her weight, snow crunching under her boots as she wraps her coat tighter around herself, trying to fight off the icy chill.

The corners of my lips curve up. I may have closed myself off from ever finding love or happiness in this new world, but Cyan's always been softer than me. Even if he's built walls of thorns around his heart.

"H-hello," he stumbles out ever so eloquently, his eyes drinking in every inch of Morana.

I knock my knee against his, rolling my eyes. "Morning, Mor," I offer a smile.

She reluctantly drags her eyes away from Cyan. "Hey, Mallrie. It's nice to see you again. How are you feeling?"

"Better, thank you," I lie easily. My absence was raising concerns for Morana. When you live in such a small town, you're bound to bump into people, so we explained to her that my immune system is compromised and I actively avoid going out to minimise the risk of illness. Although it felt like a ridiculous and improbable excuse, she accepted it, and now she frequently prepares chicken noodle soup for me when I'm feeling unwell.

Morana pulls her red scarf from inside her coat and wraps it around my neck. "Wouldn't want you catching a cold," she says, and I have to stifle a chuckle.

"You're very sweet. It's nice to know Cyan has someone looking out for him."

"Yeah, well, Mor is right. We don't want you to get *sick* again. Why don't you go get us a hot drink?" Cyan grumbles, which causes Morana to struggle to reign in her smile. It's nice to know that she enjoys his grumpy ass.

I can't help the smirk pulling at my lips as I fold my half of the paper and drop it into Cyan's lap. "I guess I'm going to go get us some coffee then," I say, offering her my seat. She blushes and slides next to Cyan, her thigh brushing against his and her hand finding his. "Would you like something, Morana?"

"A hot chocolate would be amazing. Thanks, Mallrie." She smiles at me briefly before her eyes find Cyan again, and the blush creeping across his face darkens. "The decorations are coming together nicely. Are you going to attend the festival?"

It isn't a question for me, so I leave Cyan to navigate the uncharted depths of his heart. I never thought I'd believe in love at first sight, but when Cyan first laid eyes on Morana, I could see something shift in his expression, those thorny walls wilting just a little around his heart. He was hesitant to start something with her, but with a little brotherly push, I think I finally did something right in my life.

Stepping into the vintage-style diner—which I enjoy so much because I particularly liked the time the owner, Sofia, has styled it around—I glance over my shoulder, where I can see Cyan and Morana through the window. The gingham print curtains frame them as Cyan leans forward and kisses Morana as she laughs at whatever it is he said.

He's finally found happiness.

Emotion clogs my throat as I turn my attention away and walk to the counter.

Sofia scoots down the counter, a small child—and namesake of her diner—pressed against her hip. Her dark curls fall from the red bandanna attempting to keep them in place. She looks flustered but still manages a warm smile as she says, "Hey, doll, what can I get you?"

CHAPTER FORTY-ONE

MALLRIE

I f two people could get even closer on a bench, Cyan and Morana figured out how, with her practically sitting in his lap. Not in a gross over-display of affection, but they've angled their bodies into each other, as if the world has just melted away. A thickness forms in my throat as guilt churns through my gut. Cyan's finally found his place in this world, finally found true happiness, and I don't want to fuck it up for him with promises we made almost a century ago.

I school my expression back into something more casual as I approach the pair. "Here you go," I say, clearing my throat.

Morana blinks at me as if she'd forgotten I was even here. "Thanks, Mallrie. What do I owe you?"

I wave my hand. "Don't worry about it. It's on me."

Cyan rolls his eyes as Mor asks if I want to join them. It takes all of my self-control not to laugh as I remember Cyan saying how kind she is, always inviting people to dinner, or to join them for lunch when all he wants is to be left alone. With Morana. "Thank you, but I think I'll go see some old friends. While I'm feeling good, that is."

"Aw, that sounds lovely. Well, see how you're feeling, but I was just saying to Cy that we should have you over for dinner soon. It's been a while since we've all caught up." There's so much hope glittering in her green eyes, and yet Cyan looks like he wishes for me to decline or just burst into flames. "Of course, you're welcome to stay in the guest room," Morana laughs. "I wouldn't expect you to leave afterwards."

Now I cannot stop myself from laughing, especially at the look of horror on Cyan's face. "I'm sure Mallrie's got better things to do with his time, baby," he says, burying his face in her neck and kissing softly. Morana swats his affections away playfully.

"Well, yeah, but I want to get to know him better. I also want to know what Cyan was like as a kid. He won't tell me anything." Mor pouts dramatically. "You'll tell me all the good, embarrassing stories, won't you?"

I tap my finger against my chin, pretending to think. "I don't think there are that many embarrassing stories about Cyan... unless you count the time he threw up all over my bed because he couldn't hold his liquor."

Morana's eyes light up. She's practically vibrating in her seat for more information. "Oh, my Gods! YES! Tell me everything." She scoots out from under Cyan's arm, resting her elbows on her knees as if she's captured by this crumb of his past.

We both burst into laughter at the look of horror on Cyan's face. "I'll see you tomorrow night. I can share some good stories then."

"Bring baby photos!" Morana calls after me at the same time Cyan curses me as I walk off, waving over my shoulder.

I genuinely like Morana. She's fun and knows how to

make Cyan laugh and *enjoy* life. I feel like our sisters would have approved of her, which makes my chest ache a little as I head across the centre of town, barely giving the Enkanti Tree a second glance as I walk past.

Jumping up the steps of the library, I push open the heavy wooden door adorned with fabricated carvings of protection. The librarians look up as I walk in, and their bodies tense. I drop my half-drunk cup onto the mahogany desk in the centre of the room and it makes a semi-hollow echo. Anger boils under my skin as my gaze falls on them. It hasn't simmered in all these years.

"Hello, there," I drawl. A knot forms in my chest like it does every damn time I see Selma Beaumont. She should be dead. She shouldn't be standing here, aged well beyond her years. She sold her people out. She used her body to manipulate Jeremiah. She was always too cunning. After the coven was burnt, she started spending more and more time with Jeremiah, like a common whore. She got herself pregnant to ensure nothing ever happened to her. Sometimes, I wonder if that was the catalyst that drove Charleston to murder my sisters and all the other witchlings.

My eyes drag away from Selma and her silver bracelets —one for each child, grandchild and great-grandchild in her bloodline who doesn't remember her pitiful existence to the other Enkantians. They've all aged well into their later stages of life, where the Fates were ready to take their hand and lead them into Vraska and the Afterlife.

But I stopped that.

I froze their *Timelines* like Cyan and myself but stripped them of their magic. They're just frozen husks of the witches they used to be, trapped here under Cyan's guard, forced to be our eyes and ears when we cannot be here.

Avark takes a step forward, leaning heavily on his

walking stick because of an injury Cyan gave him. I smile at the memory of Cyan telling me how Avark begged for death as he shattered his leg with a metal rod. At least now he's got a reason for the cane he was always so fond of.

"You are not welcome here, Mallrie." His voice is grave yet soft, like the leather books surrounding them.

I click my tongue. "But this is a public space." His eyes bore into me as if he could make me spontaneously combust. I shake my head. "I think you'll find that my brother and I will go wherever we please. Especially after we found out *you* were the one who told Charleston how to weaken our coven."

Avark's mouth opens and closes like a fish out of water. "I-I... Mallrie, you need to understand—"

I wave my hand, silencing him. "Save it, Avark. You've tried to explain for fifty years. And every time, you're only making the idea of driving my blade through you and trapping your soul forever all that more enticing." There's a look of resignation on his face as if he wishes for that too.

"What do you want, Mallrie?" Selma asks, her long grey hair braided down her back.

My lip curls back at her casual tone. "I'm here to see if you have any news for me." Five pairs of eyes drop to the rich wood. "Nothing?" I ask in disbelief.

"Well..." starts Zaelfe. "The mayor's son has been in here... *a lot.*"

I shake my head, "And? He's the son of the mayor. A journalist major. He enjoys reading." I also knew this. Cyan has mentioned it before.

Zaelfe shakes his head. "He is *reading* the journals. Making notes." My brows press together.

"It appears he's trying to fill in the... *blanks,*" Zaelfe

whispers, as if he's afraid Charleston himself will rise from the Afterlife and pull him back with him.

I keep my expression neutral as I say, "See, was that so hard?" Picking up my coffee and turning on my heel, I stalk out of the library.

I need to look into the *Timeline* and figure out what Edgar is planning.

I need to talk to Cyan.

I find him where I left him with Morana, but the latter is nowhere to be seen. "Where's your girlfriend?" I tease.

His cheeks burn bright pink, and even the tips of his ears colour with embarrassment. "She's not my girlfriend," he grinds out between clenched teeth, not because he's angry, but because he's trying to reign in the grin, trying to pull at the corner of his lips. She is most definitely his girlfriend, even if he's afraid to put a label on it all these months later.

"Mm," I hum, smiling smugly.

I'm happy for him, truly. I have only ever wanted my brother to be happy, healthy and *safe*. And for the first time in decades, he's smiling. Those smiles are the only thing making me smile, so I don't continue to tease him. "Will she be back?" I ask, my tone dropping into a more serious octave.

Cyan's dark brows press together. "No, she had to get back to work. She was just on her lunch break." I nod, draining the last of my coffee. "Why? You two want to compare embarrassing stories?" There's a hint of concern in his voice.

"I have a feeling we should take a look at the *Timeline* now."

CHAPTER FORTY-TWO

CYAN

1986

The minutes flick by on the computer monitor, and yet I still favour checking my watch to be certain the time is correct. There's a small black-and-white photograph poking out from the top of my keyboard. My smile fades as I slide it back into its hiding place as the sound of footsteps approaches. I need to leave in ten minutes to meet Mallrie, so whoever is approaching my too-small cubicle better talk fast.

"Hey, Cyan, you got a moment?" Edgar McQuoid Junior slides into the already too cramped space, sitting on my desk.

I look back down at my watch, at the second hand constantly ticking. "I've got to meet someone in ten for lunch, soooo..." I draw out the word, trying to let him come to his own conclusions.

"Yeah, yeah. I think this is a little more exciting than meeting the missus." Edgar's brown hair is parted in its usual way, off to the side. His grey eyes are alight with amusement.

"It's not... I'm meeting my brother." The words tumble out of my mouth. I've been dancing on the edge of a double-edged sword for months now, befriending Edgar. I need to tell him enough about my life that I seem interesting and trustworthy but not enough that he finds me *too* interesting.

"Mallrie? When do I get to meet your mysterious brother?"

I chuckle under my breath. *Never, if I can help it.* "Maybe another day. He's just gotten over one of his 'colds,'" I say, air quoting the word and rolling my eyes. Edgar too bought the lie we spun around Mallrie's disappearances.

"Whatever. This is more exciting, anyway." Edgar pushes the paperwork and my keyboard aside, and I scramble to catch the photograph and slip it into my pocket before he can see it. His excitement blinds him from what's happening around him, and I crane my neck to make sure our lieutenant isn't near enough to catch us. "I found this in the Library." Edgar folds out a piece of paper that's been photocopied from a book.

My head twists to the side. "First," I ask, running my hand across the page of familiar writing. "How the fuck did you get this?" I don't need to elaborate. There are no photocopiers in the library, and they strictly forbid the journals from leaving the building.

Edgar winks at me. "I snuck it out. Brought it here. Photocopied it. Then returned it." He punctuates the words, his voice filled with cunning pride that makes my skin crawl.

I open and close my mouth, feigning that I don't know

exactly what I am looking at. "What is this? What am I meant to be looking at?"

"Here, look." Edgar points to an inkblot that Mallrie and I carefully censored years ago. Too many people knew about the journals to simply destroy them all. Plus, Mallrie always thought it'd be good to have them in case we ever needed to convince the people of Datura about the truth of the past. "You can't see it too well 'cause of the photocopy, *but* that inkblot doesn't belong there!"

"Edgar..." I start, craning my neck around the walls of my small cubicle, now hoping that the lieutenant will stumble upon us. "I think you're overthinking that. That book is, what, centuries old? They were probably writing with fucking mud and bird feathers," I scoff, and I imagine what Hesper would say.

Edgar just looks at me smugly, as if he knows something I don't. "Don't believe me? Look at this," he says, pulling out another page. My stomach does a flip as—faintly—I can see the word *'Faerie'* written in Charleston's immaculate script.

I shake my head, pretending I don't know what's written there.

"Faerie, Cyan. It says *Faerie."*

I scoff again, tapping my paperwork about the disappearance of a woman on top of the photocopies Edgar brought in. "I don't think that means what you think it means."

Again, there's a knowing gleam in his eye. "Yeah?" he asks, shifting his weight and pulling something out of his pocket. "What do you think of this?" His voice drops to a conspiratorial whisper, and the way he looks around before handing me the photograph has my stomach in knots.

CHAPTER FORTY-THREE

MALLRIE

I arch a brow in the large misnac's direction as she defiantly holds her paw, claws extended towards the glass panel. We both know that she could easily just slip through the wall if she so wished, but she's doing this on purpose. I hold her gaze. Her feline eyes blink once, revealing blood-red pupils before blinking away. "Don't start," I warn, pointing my finger at her.

Winnie could easily slip through the closed door. She could easily appear right in front of me and start to maul me. But she doesn't. Instead, she retracts her claws and starts pacing in front of the glass-panelled doors, her tail an angry swish behind her. It has me remembering that small misnac that Cyan and I found, scared, alone and almost frozen to death. Once Winnie had regained some of her strength, she stalked much like this in front of me for hours on end, four red eyes hardly blinking, barely looking away from me as she paced. Wondering whether or not she could trust me, I suppose. Eventually, she realised that I was the one sneaking half-dead squirrels into the room for her, and she warmed up more.

I guess it's that memory—that the Fates gave me something else to look after once Cyan was grown and wanted to spend time on his own than with his older brother—that has me sighing and walking back towards the house. My formative years were spent caring for a child no one else wanted. When Cyan no longer needed me, I felt lost, but then we found Winnie. And now, I think I need her more than she knows. Or maybe she does know. Maybe she knows how hard it is for me to go months without seeing Cyan. Perhaps she knows that fleeting moments here and there are not enough for me when he's always been less than a room away. Maybe she can sense the black hole of loneliness that's carved in my chest where my heart is meant to be since Charleston murdered Alinta, Adriana and Abeline.

As I slide down and rest my head against the cool glass pane, my throat burns with the memories of their names. As I hear Winnie's tiny whine, my already-wounded heart aches even more. "Win, please." Sadness laces every syllable. *This isn't fair to her. This isn't how she should be living.* "You know why I can't let you come with me."

The large misnac makes a throaty purring sound.

"Cyan will be home in three days for dinner." There's a shudder of magic and the glass pane bends beneath my forehead as Winnie slips through the door. Her large paws rest in my lap as she licks the finger I pointed at her. "I'm sorry, Win." I bury my face in the fur of her neck and inhale deeply. Memories come flooding back to me of my sisters, a small ball of spotted fur curled up in Adriana's lap, and Alinta and Abeline showering the tiny creature with so much love and affection. My grip tightens in her coat, and I fall onto my ass, a sob breaking free.

Winnie nudges at my chest, and reluctantly, I let her go.

Leaning against the door frame, my grief rips through me, my body shuddering with each heart-wrenching sob. Winnie climbs into my lap—no longer the tiny misnac— her head resting on my shoulder. I wrap my arms around her body, and my throat burns. "I failed them, Win. I f- failed them," I sob loudly. "Just like I failed Cyan. I can't do this. I couldn't protect my brother against *Father*. I couldn't protect my coven–*fuck*. Winnie, I was to become the High Witch. How was I meant to protect an entire coven when I couldn't even protect my brother?"

I'm exhausted. Years spent waiting, trying to rebuild a relationship with Cyan. Trying to protect the people of Datura from the Kailadons. Making sure Amos, Caspian, Selma, Avark and Zaelfe didn't expose all of our secrets and ruin everything. Trying to hunt down our mother's grimoire that Charleston took, or any grimoire or anything else that belonged to our coven.

And for *what?*

I am still no closer than when we started. All I know is that I need to wait for the one born with both Fae and elemental magic running through their veins, and that their sacrifice will be the key to restoring the magic. The latter I left out when informing Cyan of what I oversaw of the Fates weaving into the *Timeline*.

My chest aches at the thought of having to spill an innocent's blood just because of my mother's hateful heart. Even worse, this child is yet to be born. I won't steal and murder a babe, but is waiting for them to mature any better?

The Fae didn't come when Cersei called to them for aid in the fight with Charleston, and for that, she seeks her revenge even in the Afterlife.

I don't want to do it. But I made a promise.

"And Delacroix always keeps their promise." My father's voice still echoes in my mind even after all these years, as if it was only yesterday he spoke those words.

"I am not a Delacroix," I seethe, tears burning my throat with every word. "I am nothing like my parents."

CHAPTER FORTY-FOUR

CYAN

"Mr Elias, a word?" I flinch, as I turn to face the lieutenant, who couldn't have worse timing. He could have interrupted Edgar's talk about the Fae scout he caught on film and the elaborate plan to catch one that he's somehow roped me into. The only reason I agreed is because he hinted at something he's been working on that has my interest piqued.

My boots click together as I straighten my posture, as was taught when I started working at the GDO. Not that it took much training. Atherton pretty much had this drilled into me by the time I could walk. "Sir?"

The lieutenant is a short and stocky man, his salt and pepper hair more salt than pepper these days. "I've been reviewing your file, and..." his voice trails off as he flips the page, reading something on the other side. I cringe at the photograph they took when I started working here, my hair slicked back and bags under my eyes from the lack of sleep while I joined Mallrie patrolling the streets, killing Kailadons—and for what?

"You've been exceeding my expectations recently," The lieutenant is saying, drawing my attention back. "If you keep this up, I can guarantee a promotion in your future."

I smile, bowing my head slightly. "Thank you, sir. You won't be disappointed."

"I hope not," He says with a knowing smile. "I'll be keeping a close eye on you. Especially now—"

"Respectively, sir?" I say, cutting him off mid-sentence. "Morana and I would like to keep our... *news* private for now."

"Very good," replies Lieutenant Thorne. Morana's mother mustn't have been able to keep her mouth shut and told her sister, who then told her husband.

I give him a tight-lipped smile and leave the GDO. It's not a long walk to our rendezvous point, but I've had enough distractions that I take the fire exit instead of the main staircase.

As I expected, Mallrie is waiting for me in Morana's and my favourite spot at Christina's Cafe. The cosy booth by the window provides a pleasant view of the Enkanti Tree and the buildings that surround it. Mallrie's back is to the door, a position I didn't expect him to take, but I also didn't expect to see his shoulders curved in on themselves.

I clap a hand on his shoulder as I approach. "Hey..." I drawl, angling my head to get a good look at his face.

"What took you so long?" Mallrie asks. The words come out quickly and hushed as he slips out of the booth to wrap his arms around me in a half-bro-hug, as Morana's cousin calls it.

I muster a smile that's buried in Mallrie's neck as I clap my hand on his shoulder. "Ah, you know how work is," I say with a wink as we pull away.

Mallrie's gaze shifts away from me to the tree in the centre of town. "Not exactly," he mutters, and I can hear the guilt in his voice.

I slide into my chair, looking out at the tree. "Is everything... *okay?*" I flinch at the word. Countless times, Mallrie or I have asked this seemingly harmless question only for one or the other to explode with years of pent-up guilt, grief and anger. Because *nothing* is okay. But maybe... my hand slides along the pocket of my slacks. Maybe that could change. "Is Winnie—"

"She's fine," Mallrie replies quickly, and I notice his throat work away the emotion in those two paltry words. "It's just..." his lips roll into his mouth, pulling tight the scar that's sliced through them. I try not to think of that day, of how it felt to slice open his face in that unchecked rage. Mallrie clears his throat, snapping my attention back to him. "It's their birthday."

Ah. "I know," I whisper, rubbing the back of my neck. Maybe now isn't the best time to share my news with him. "I was wondering if I could come—"

"I'd love that," Mallrie says, finally looking at me with glass-covered eyes. He's been looking after the aeimweriah, and he's been doing a good job, but I still don't trust him after all this time not to rip out the wrong plant.

We sit in silence for a long time. Sofia comes placing two cups of coffee before us, Christina following not far behind her, pushing two plastic cups onto the table before following her mother away in her matching uniform, tripping over her feet in her rush to keep pace.

"I failed them," Mallrie whispers, his hands wrapped around the ceramic mug. But his eyes never leave the Enkanti Tree—*Vaasis*. His eyes have a purple shimmer to them, and I know his magic is dragging him back to the past, drowning him in his self-loathing and grief. "I can't... I can't do this."

The words aren't meant for me, but I reach across the table, squeezing his arm anyway. A small gesture. Hopefully, he knows I am here for him, even if I don't know how to voice it.

"There was..." My mouth feels like it's been stuffed with cotton as I try to speak the words that I once threw in his face. "There was nothing you could do." Mallrie lifts his gaze to me at my words, a dark eyebrow inching up his forehead. "Don't give me that look," I grouse, pulling my hand away.

"Why? When you've spent so much time telling me that I *should* have done more?"

His words aren't meant to be cruel. Over the decades that have passed, our relationship has ebbed and flowed. There is so much hurt and shared pain that I don't know if we'll ever have a normal relationship. Not something Morana would understand. My hand travels below the table to my pocket once more, and fear builds in my chest at the news I need to share with him. *What will Mallrie think? That I'm foolish for getting myself into this situation. Will he be scared?*

I roll my bottom lip between my teeth and bite down. "It's just as you've said hurtful words to me in the past, too." I scratch my brow. This isn't how I wanted this conversation to go. "But we *will do this,* Mallrie. I promise.

I'll help you restore the magic. Keep the promise you made to our mother. Avenge the deaths of our sisters and coven."

"Revenge gets you nowhere, brother. Haven't you learnt that by now? Look at Charleston. The *librarians*." Mallrie scoffs at our nickname for them. "Every soul I have slayed with my sword..." His face scrunches up with disgust. "So much revenge... and for what? I don't feel any better. The next day is the same."

I lean back and cross one knee over the other, shrugging nonchalantly. "One less piece of shit soul on the earth." *A brighter future for us.*

Mallrie snorts a laugh. "Well, that's true."

We sit silently for a moment, enjoying the quiet and the coffee. Sofia returns to refill our cups, to which bright-eyed Christina peers over the edge of the table. "Wou didn't like the cawfee?" she says in the way only a four-year-old can, jumbling the words into a somewhat coherent mess.

We smile at her. "It was delicious," I say, receiving a slitted-eye look from Christina while Mallrie animatedly takes a sip of the plastic cup, asking if he can have some more. Sofia apologises for Christina as she takes our order and returns to the kitchen.

"You're so much better at that than me," I say, feeling a flutter of anxiety migrate from my chest to my stomach.

Mallrie shrugs. "Kids just want to feel included."

I look down at the red-and-white-printed napkin, attempting to smooth out the crinkles. "Mm? Any other advice?" I ask, feeling the heat on my cheeks.

"Um..."

I dare to look up at his quizzical look. "You're going to be an uncle." The words tumble out of my mouth and Mallrie just sits there and blinks at me. Panic starts to settle in my bones, and I run my sweaty hand over my pocket where the weird alien photograph sits.

"I'm... what?" Mallrie's brows pinch in confusion and I pull out the strange photograph, as if that'll clear this up. It doesn't, since Mallrie doesn't know what an uncle is because we've never had a word for it. He doesn't know what he's looking at.

"See that weird-looking bean?" I ask as Mallrie twists the photograph upside down, to which I correct. Morana had to show me nearly ten times the correct way to hold it, and since then, I've marked a small dot in the bottom right-hand corner. "That... that's my kid."

Mallrie's eyes widen almost comically as he looks from the black-and-white photograph to me and back. "Are you serious?" he breathes.

I nod, tears flooding my vision.

"Oh, Cyan. I am so happy for you, brother." Mallrie pulls me from my chair and wraps his arms around me in a punishing grip that knocks the air from my lungs.

We take our seats just as Sofia comes to the table. "Well, I hope these are happy tears," she says, placing extra napkins on the table.

Mallrie chuckles, rubbing his cheek with the back of his hand as I say, "Yeah, just telling my brother that he's going to be an uncle." He was the last person on our list of people to tell. May as well let the whole fucking town know now. If you want news to spread, drop it at Christina's. Sofia will have it spread faster than the *Datura Chronicles*.

Sofia's big brown eyes widen as she looks from me to Mallrie. "Oh, congratulations! That's so exciting! How far along is Morana?"

"About four months." I can never keep up. It's all too surreal. When Mallrie froze our *Timelines*, I just assumed that... *that* would cease from working too. "We're off to the practitioner this afternoon for another scan."

"Well, coffee is on me today," Sofia says, smiling. "No wonder Morana has been in here, ordering up all my waffles." She knocks her elbow against my shoulder. "She'll be sending you broke soon, with her cravings."

CHAPTER FORTY-FIVE
CYAN

My eyes narrow as I jab Mallrie in the shoulder, my voice filled with warning as I growl. "Don't you fucking dare!" I turn my eyes back to the narrow street, slowing my steps so he can lead as we walk in single file, allowing the flow of people past. "We do this together," I hiss into his ear.

Mallrie stops suddenly, pulling me into an alcove, his hand running over his face like he does when he's getting a headache—one that usually forms because of his magic trying to force itself to the surface. I've given him shit in the past about it, but it seems to be quite taxing for him. Even if he doesn't tell me exactly how draining it is. "It's just, with Morana being with child now..."

Laughter rips from my throat, causing Mallrie to stop talking and glare at me. Sucking in a breath of stale air, I raise my hands in defence but another wave of hysteria crawls up my throat. "Sorry," I chuckle, composing myself. "It's just that people don't talk like that anymore, mate. Just say she's pregnant."

Mallrie just rolls his eyes. "I just don't want anything to

happen to her. To either of you or the baby." Mallrie's eyes drop and I shove my hand in my pocket just to feel the crumble of paper against my skin, to know that this is real. "You're too close to this," he says. "I don't like that Edgar *Junior* is looking into the past."

I bite my tongue and my stomach clenches. I'm keeping what Edgar has just told me about the Fae from Mallrie. He's got enough to deal with. I can handle this. As I clap a hand on his shoulder, I can feel the strength and solidity of his muscles, but this is something he doesn't need to carry on his own. "Neither do I, but like I said, we're in this together. Delacroix's and promises and all of that shit." I wave a hand in the air. I try not to think about Atherton— and all the shit I had to endure from him—too much these days.

Now it's Mallrie's turn to chuckle. "I thought you didn't go by that name anymore?" His eyes shine as he arches an eyebrow.

Bastard. I smile. "Yeah, well, some of Atherton's lessons still stick."

His smile fades. Suddenly, his boots are more interesting than monitoring the Antique store across the alleyway. "Are you afraid?" he asks. "About becoming like him?"

I shake my head. "Actually, he's kind of like the best parenting book I can get my hands on." A crooked smile tugs at my lips. "I just do the exact opposite of everything *he* did." We laugh together, and it feels good. "Besides," I say, knocking Mallrie's shoe with my own, "I had the best big brother. He taught me everything I need to know... and... I hope he'll be around to keep teaching me."

A strangled sound comes from the back of Mallrie's throat. "Of course," he says. "It'd be an *honour.*"

We stand in silence for a few minutes, Mallrie looking

at the photograph of Morana and my child, a small smile tugging at the corner of his lips. "Are you going to tell Mor about your... *gifts?*"

"Eventually," I sigh. "I don't think she needs that stress right now."

Mallrie nods, and I'm sure he's wondering how that conversation could potentially play out. *"Hey babe, how's the baby? Doing anything strange recently? No? Well, let me know if the plants start growing wildly, because the baby may have something to do with it."*

"Are you sure this is where you saw her?" The shadows grow long on the sidewalk. I've never feared being out after dark. Death has always been a constant companion, but now I have something *good* in my life, something that has me excited to wake up each morning. I don't want to tempt the Fates.

"This is the shop," Mallrie confirms. "Do you have to go?" he asks as he notices me checking my watch.

Shaking my head, I say, "I've got time." I smirk at him as his face slackens with the annoyance of hearing my new favourite joke. Ever since Charleston's descendants created these timepieces, I've been starting shit with Mallrie that I also possess time.

"You're not funny," he says, but I can see the smile stretching that scar I gave him so long ago.

I open my mouth to remark, but the door to the antique shop opens, bells jingling merrily. A woman steps outside, her belly swollen. Her husband wraps his arms around her growing waist, pulling her closer. My chest aches with the thought of someday soon being unable to wrap my arms around Morana, of the child that will crawl between us in the middle of the night because of a bad dream. How Mor will sing them back to sleep and I'll hold them so close that they'll know that nothing will ever harm them.

Mallrie stalks off in the opposite direction to the couple, and it takes me a moment to shake my daydream and catch up to him. "This is so fucked up," he's mumbling to himself.

"Mal, wait, slow down! What's going on?" I ask, pushing past people to catch up to him.

"My vision must be wrong." His lips press into a thin line, and I know he's lying to me.

"Your visions are never *wrong*," I say, pulling him to a stop and off to the side. "They *change*. We don't know if it'll change, or shift, or whatever the fuck the Fates do to fuck with us. But they're there. We're on the right track, yeah?"

"How do you *think* they become part-Fae?" Mallrie grits between his teeth.

A shudder works its way down my spine. *The Fae. The photograph.* My thumb traces across my lip as all that Edgar's been telling me finally starts to fall into place. I clear my throat. "Maybe it's just a gift of the Fates," I say, trying to keep my tone even. "A coincidence."

Mallrie scoffs. "When have you ever believed in coincidences? The Fates are so obsessed with controlling every fracture of the future that there's no room for them."

I blink. I didn't know Mallrie knew that much about the Fates. He's never shared it with me. But I guess I was never privy to what went on in that cave. I muster an easy smile on my face. "I don't think something sinister is going on behind closed doors, Mal." *Oh, there most certainly is.* "If there was, I'd know."

Mallrie doesn't look convinced, but if Edgar wants to fuck around with the Fae—and if whatever he's got planned will lead towards the magic being restored—I'll do it. I'll help the power-hungry bastard so that Morana and my child can live in a town where they don't need to fear for their safety every night.

"That child is going to be our salvation, Mallrie," I say, a wave of conflicting emotions coursing through me, but I push them aside as I grip the photograph in my pocket.

He looks at me, and for the first time since we murdered Atherton, he's got that mask on again—the one where I cannot decipher what that emotion is behind his eyes. "That they will be." Mallrie's jaw tightens with words he's not speaking, but I clap him on the back.

Whatever it is, he's not wanting to speak aloud. I cannot fault him.

After all, we all have our secrets.

GLOSSARY

Aeimweriah - An elemental shrine to those who have been lost. Generally, aeimweriah are gardens but can also be bowls/vessels of water or an altar of candles.

Ashga - Seven-foot-tall, long pointed ears, bony fingers, glowing golden eyes. Generally friendly. "Doesn't usually enjoy the taste of flesh" -Mallrie.

Enkantian - A coven of witches that possess elemental magic. (Fire, Earth, Water, Air and Time.)

High Witchess - The leader of the Enkantian coven. The High Witchess swears an oath to protect all those in their coven and harnesses a kernel of all elemental magics which they use to perform the Vaasis Ritual.

Kailadon (Flesh-Hunter) - A large nocturnal flesh-eating monster. The Kailadon is unnaturally tall and skinny, a thin layer of reddish-brown flesh stretching across its bones. The Kailadon is faceless save for two slits for a nose and a large mouth that stretches from where one ear would be to the other. This mouth peels open as if someone is slowly unzipping it revealing needle point teeth. The Kailadon's arms are long and pointed like two knives and deadly sharp, perfect for slicing off their prey's skin to consume. Charleston and his people refer to these creatures as Flesh-Hunters because of their insatiable hunger.

Lorkreig - A species of elves that live deep within the Melsheim Forest, their magic is deeply connected with the earth. Their magic allows them to be able to manipulate the earth but also to summon it like the Enkantian witches.

Meshlynk - A large and vicious creature that hunts for sport. Its body is covered in moss and shrubbery giving it the perfect camouflage within the Melsheim Forest. It has long claws that extend from its fingertips and stag antlers protrude from its head. The shrubbery that is growing from its body also acts as a hood protecting its skull. The Meshlynk will flip back this hood to expose its grey skull and glowing red eyes. If one looks into a Meshlynk's eyes too long the creature can dig into your mind and take control.

Mishk - Beautiful but deadly.

Misnac - A large magical cat that is now extinct (except for Winnifred.) The large cats are usually tanned with black spots, with large ears and claws. Micnacs are very loyal creatures, once serving those of royal blood. The large cats possess magic which is why they were hunted due to the witches' jealousy.

Nechkrappe - Notorious tricksters, creatures of destruction and chaos the Nechkrappe is a large black bird similar to a raven but with milky white eyes making the creature appear blind. Nechkrappe's can harness dark magic that is unknown to many as one who encounters a Nechkrappe usually doesn't last long enough to study their magic.

Vaasis (Enkanti Tree) - Large Oak tree at the centre of the Enkantian Coven which holds the magic of the witches and Fae to protect the Enkantians. Vaasis is later renamed the

Enkani Tree by Albert Charleston as a reminder of the deaths of the witches.

Vraska - The place between life and death. The Fae watch over Vraska and make sure the souls travel to the correct Afterlife.

Wyntesstval - The winter festival celebrated by the Enkantian witches on the longest night of the year. It's a time where they believe the Fates are not meddling with the *Timeline,* and so the witches stop to celebrate and give thanks for all the Fates have gifted them that year.

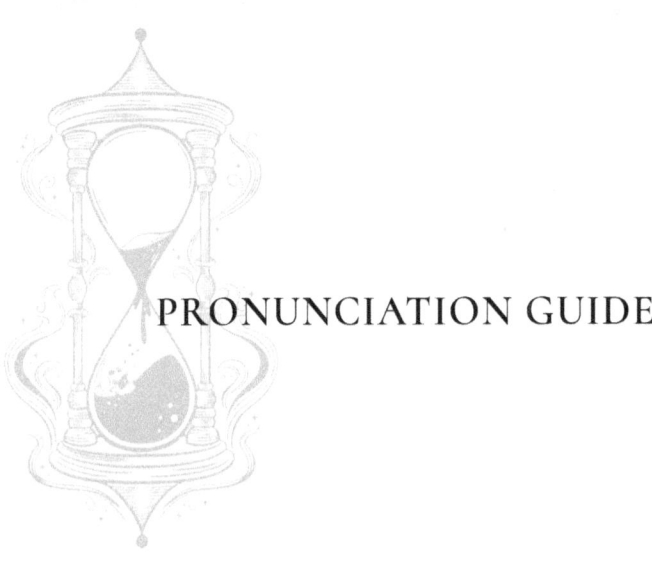

PRONUNCIATION GUIDE

People

Mallrie – mall-ree
Cyan – ky-anne
Atherton – ath-er-ton
Cersei – suh-see
Delacroix – duh-luh-kwaa
Avark – a-v-arc
Azalea – uh-zay-lee-uh
(Edgar) MacQuoid – mack-koid

Species

Enkantian – en-can-tee-an
Kailadon – kai-la-don
Meshlynk – mesh-link
Ashga – ash-ga
Misnac – mi-s-nac
Lorkreig – lor-kri-geg
Nechkrappe – ne-ssh-crap

Places

Datura – duh-chuor-ruh
Vraska – v-ras-ka
Melsheim (Forest) – mel-shh-em

ACKNOWLEDGMENTS

I can't believe we're here yet again! Writing FALL OF THE WITCHES was an absolute journey! I've heard that authors struggle to write the second book in a series, so I thought I was so clever in writing a prequel but boy, was I wrong! What was meant to be a novella (once again) spiralled and is now a full-length novel, and like I said in my acknowledgments in RISE OF THE WITCHES, it takes a village to write a book and I am so grateful to be surrounded by so many amazing people that helped make this book in your hands (whether that be a paperback or eBook) possible.

First and foremost, a massive thank you to my husband, Alex, for his continued love and support and never wavering belief in me and my ability to write, even when the imposter gremlin would keep me up at night riddling me with self doubt. And my dad for continuing to bring to life the most terrifying monsters that pop into my head.

To my Beta Readers, THANK YOU for being the best support, helping shape FOTW and for your words of encouragement. I know I wasn't the most active in the comments, but your little notes meant everything to me and really spurred me on in the developmental edits stage.

To Brittany, my wonderful editor and cheerleader, thank you for your amazing work polishing FOTW to really make her shine. I've absolutely loved working with you and cannot wait to continue working with you.

Again, thank you to Dom and the team at 3 Crows Author Services for creating such a stunning cover!

Finally, to my readers, every single one of you, thank you! Thank you from the bottom of my heart for your love and support for this indie author. Thank you for taking a chance on me and my book, and I hope you enjoyed it as much as I enjoyed creating it.

ABOUT THE AUTHOR

Melissa lives in Brisbane, Australia with her husband Alex and their two children, Emily and Oskar.

With an active imagination that can sometimes get her in trouble for imagining up unrealistic situations, and a joke made between Alex and Melissa on a rare childless night out back in November 2021, Melissa embarked on the journey of writing her own book.

Melissa loves to spend time with her family but also enjoys curling up on the couch exploring new worlds as she reads a variety of books from different genres.

To stay up to date on new releases and bonus bookish content you can follow Melissa on Instagram or sign up to her newsletter at https://www.mljewellauthor.com.au/

ALSO BY M.L JEWELL

Rise of the Witches is available on Amazon, KindleUnlimited

Signed paperbacks are available through M.L Jewell's website.

https://www.mljewellauthor.com.au/shop/signedbooks